D0335657

Ric

Please renew or return items by the date shown on your receipt

www.hertfordshire.gov.uk/libraries

Renewals and enquiries: 0300 123 4049

Textphone for hearing or 0300 123 4041 speech impaired users:

L32 11.16

CAMILLA CHESTER

—

Matador
9 Priory Business Park,
Wistow Road, Kibworth Beauchamp,
Leicestershire. LE8 0RX
Tel: 0116 279 2299
Email: books@troubador.co.uk
Web: www.troubador.co.uk/matador
Twitter: @matadorbooks

ISBN 978 1788032 520

British Library Cataloguing in Publication Data.
A catalogue record for this book is available from the British Library.

Printed and bound in the UK by TJ International, Padstow, Cornwall
Typeset in 11.5pt Aldine401 BT by Troubador Publishing Ltd, Leicester, UK

Matador is an imprint of Troubador Publishing Ltd.

Chapter One

Dinners To Die For Competition

On the slightly smelly sofa, in the run-down common room of Brocken House, Lucas Larks sat transfixed by the TV. The screen was filled by celebrity chef, Leonardo De'Largio. Bulging out of his dinner jacket, his white-streaked hair combed up and back with waxy grease, the chef looked like a fat badger. Lucas thought Leonardo was the greatest, because no matter how much cheese Lucas ate he would never, ever be as big as him.

The famous chef had a weird way of talking. It

was his Italian accent, but sometimes he muddled up words too. Lucas liked that he wasn't perfect.

'It is competition time,' Leonardo boomed.

A competition on *Dinners to Die For*? *This could be awesome*, thought Lucas.

'Budge up Larks, you big fatty,' said Tucker elbowing Lucas in the ribs.

'Shut it, Turkey,' Lucas snapped back, shifting over a bit to make room for his best mate. 'Can't you see the Big Man is talking?' He jabbed a pink thumb at the telly, '*Dinners to Die For* is doing a competition.'

Tucker went quiet and stared at the screen.

'It's time for you to show us what you can do,' Leonardo continued. The other two celebrity chefs that starred on the show were standing behind Leonardo, nodding their heads. 'Two lucky winners who enter the best short film showing themselves making their own *Dinner to Die For* will come to Mouthful Mansions, to cook with all of us for a whole weekend.'

Lucas's stomach churned. This was it!

'If we like you, and you make tasty food, then it's off to Rome for a place at the Culinary School where you will learn all the trick of the trade and become real chefs.'

Lucas tried to jump up, but he was sort of wedged into the sofa. There was a rocking, wriggling effort which knocked the cat, FB to the floor. FB glared at the boys then stalked off to the corner of the common room to lick at his behind. Lucas, now standing, punched the air with his notepad.

'Yes!' he shouted. Leonardo De'Largio had just given him his chance of getting out of Brocken House.

2

Nobody was going to adopt some boring, pudgy eleven-year-old boy without freckles or dimples or anything cute. He'd been waiting forever for a family. Forget it; this was his big chance.

'Did you hear him, Larks?' Tucker's black face looked all stretched and excited. 'He said *two* lucky winners.'

'But, you're not a cook,' Lucas pointed out.

Tucker didn't even blink. 'So? Can't be that hard; you can teach me, we can blag it…we could get out of here!' He stood up from the sofa and got really close to Lucas's face. 'We could be Italian chefs. It would be brilliant.'

Lucas wondered how he could tell his best mate that he was the worse cook in the entire universe and had no chance of winning. It was hard when Tucker's eyes looked all bright and playful, like a puppy's. Maybe he could have a go at teaching him? It would be good to do it together, but Tucker was hopeless. From the telly in the background came the ending theme music from *Dinners to Die For:* Da, de dah, dah de de dah dah.

'But…but…you boiled the eggs dry,' Lucas said, at last.

'What? When?' Tucker stepped back from his friend, stuck his lip out.

'The other day, you only had to hard-boil some eggs and when I came back the pan was scorched dry.'

'Crankshaft was on!' Tucker said, outraged. 'I can't be standing there watching some boring old eggs bouncing about in a pan when Gordon Stanley is heading for terminal velocity can I? Nobody would miss an episode of Crankshaft for a few stupid eggs.'

'I would,' Lucas said.

'Forget the eggs,' Tucker said holding up his palms. 'Let's just make the entry together, yeah? It'll be awesome. You can do it all. You be Director, or whatever, I'll be your assistant…'

'Commis chef,' Lucas said.

'Whatie?'

Lucas sighed, Tucker was taking the edge off his excitement. 'Commis chef,' he explained. 'That's what it's called when you assist the Head Chef.'

'Okay,' Tucker said and grinned. 'I'll be the commis.' He laughed then. He laughed so much his belly wobbled.

'Shush you two, I want to watch this,' said Miss Downs.

They'd forgotten she was sitting there in that funny green chair; her face was peeking round the side of one of the wings. It was only really Miss Downs and Lucas that liked *Dinners to Die For*. Tucker only watched it to see what Lucas might make for his tea. She looked at the boys with her 'fake cross face' then turned back to the screen.

They both went quiet for a minute and watched the telly. It was the news. The story was something about people bringing endangered animals into the country. Lucas wasn't really listening, he was busy thinking about the competition. Tucker got bored of the news quickly. He nudged Lucas and pointed over at FB who was washing his face.

'From bum to face,' he said, in what he thought was a quiet voice but was really a sort of snorty whisper that was just as loud as before. 'Flea Bag is disgusting.'

'FB doesn't stand for Flea Bag,' Lucas whispered back. 'He's called Fire Ball and he loves me the best.'

'Who cares who he loves? He's a stinky Flea Bag.'

'Fire Ball.'

FB ignored them. He was washing his face so hard it made his orange stripes go all wonky. Lucas loved animals, all animals. There was something completely amazing and trusting about them. If he could, he would rescue every last one of them and fill the home with pets, but FB was all they had. Nobody knew what FB stood for; it was stitched in his collar when he turned up at Brocken House. Like the kids, he had nowhere better to go, so he stayed.

'Flea Bag,' said Tucker.

'Fire Ball.'

'I can still hear you,' said Miss Downs.

She may have been the best care worker at the home, but she was still a pain.

'Why don't you go and make a start on your competition film if you're going to enter?' She checked her watch. 'You've got an hour or so before bed. There's an old camcorder in the staff cupboard.' She rummaged into a pocket. 'Here's the key, don't forget to bring it back.'

Tucker mouthed 'Camcorder?' at Lucas, who shrugged in response.

Tucker grinned at his friend over his shoulder as he went to take the key that Miss Downs was holding up. Lucas grinned back. He didn't know the first thing about cooking, but there was no better mate than Tucker, they had to enter together.

Chapter Two
Camcorder and Flymo

'There's tons of junk in here,' said Tucker. He backed out of the cupboard. A grey cobweb was stuck to his hair but Lucas didn't bother telling him.

'Let me look.'

Tucker was right, there were boxes and boxes of stuff. Lucas shifted them about until he saw what had to be the camcorder. It was a massive, silver, square rectangle with a lens, a few enormous buttons and a strap. Lucas pulled it out of the cupboard and laid it on the carpet between them.

'What century is that from?' Tucker's face was all crumpled up.

Lucas shrugged. It looked so ancient he wasn't

sure if *Dinners To Die For* would accept a film made on it as a proper competition entry.

Tucker got on his knees and examined it, like he was preparing the thing for an operation. He pushed a few of the huge buttons on the top. The side of the machine sprung open fast and made such a noise that Tucker leapt up again. 'It's alive,' he squawked.

The boys stared at it from above.

'What the heck is this?' Lucas pulled out a huge black box from inside it.

'It's…its baby,' said Tucker.

That cracked them up.

'Brian Tucker and Lucas Larks, what are you up to?'

The boys jumped at the sounds of their names even though they weren't doing anything wrong. Mrs Corneal, who ran the home, stood in the doorway peering over her glasses at them.

'Miss Downs said we could use this to record our film for the *Dinners to Die For* competition,' Lucas explained, waving the black box in the air.

'I see.' She walked a couple of steps nearer. 'Well, you'll need to make sure you're not recording over anything important.'

Lucas looked at Tucker for an interpretation but he just shrugged back to say he had no clue what she was on about either.

Mrs Corneal sighed. 'It's a video tape,' she said, as if that would mean something. 'What does the label say?'

Lucas turned the box over and read it out: 'Brocken House Tour, 1994.'

'Oh well…now let me see.' She opened one of

the boxes on the floor. 'Ah, here we go.' She pulled out another enormous silver machine with a couple of black wires hanging out the back. 'You'll need to connect this bit to the television.' She waggled one of the cords at them that had three coloured ends. 'And plug it in, pop the tape in, press play and it should come up on the screen.'

The whole thing sounded like a proper headache.

'Miss Downs is watching the news,' Tucker said.

'I'm sure she won't mind. It'll be a little trip down memory lane.'

Mrs Corneal smiled and walked smartly out of the room, the wires trailing after her. Tucker picked up the camcorder and the boys followed.

It took forever, but eventually between them Miss D and Mrs C got the stupid thing working. The screen flickered into life. It was pathetic really: a wobbly tour of the house both boys knew far too well already.

'Boring,' Tucker mouthed at Lucas, who totally agreed.

'That's you Mrs Corneal,' Miss Downs practically squealed and pointed at the TV. 'You look so young.'

'Well, my hair's not grey, but what was I wearing?'

Lucas rolled his eyes at Tucker. 'So, can we record over it?' he asked them.

'What? No, go and look in the boxes for a blank tape,' said Mrs Corneal waving a dismissive hand at him. 'You can't record over Brocken House history.'

Tucker and Larks went back to pulling stuff out of

the boxes, broken bits of grown-up chat and giggles floating down the corridor towards them.

'This place never changes,' Tucker complained.

'I know, same stuff, every day. I'm sick of this house.'

'Never thought I'd want to get back to school, but I do. Summer holidays are boring. Everything is so old here. We don't even get phones! It's rubbish.'

'It should be called Broken Home, not Brocken House, look at all this old busted-up stuff.' Lucas held up an ugly-looking vase with a chip out of the top.

'Beautiful,' joked Tucker.

'And none of the nice kids stay,' Lucas said, putting the vase back. 'We're just left with Flymo.'

'Who said you could use my name?'

There he was, Flymo (named after his failed world record attempt to eat a dismantled lawnmower): the scariest boy in the universe.

'Oh my God', whispered Tucker, 'you summoned him from Hell.'

Lucas shot Tucker a look, 'You seriously need to work on your whispering technique.'

Flymo liked the idea of being summoned from Hell; he smiled, but it wasn't friendly, 'What are you two fatties up to? Must be something to do with grub.' He started swaggering towards them, clenching his hands into fists.

Lucas didn't want to tell him anything. Tucker went back to looking through boxes.

'How did you get in the staff cupboard? Been picking locks again?'

Lucas held up the key in what he hoped was a brave way, 'Miss Downs gave it to us.'

'Miss Downs gave it to us,' Flymo sang back at the younger, smaller, boy. 'Right couple of foodie thieves. Do you know what they do to thieves in some other countries?'

Lucas didn't want to know, so he went back to the boxes. Tucker had practically climbed into the cupboard; he was so desperate to get away from Flymo.

'They chop off their hands with a massive machete. No messing. Wham! Bet they never nick nothing after that, eh?'

'Can't do if they've got no hands,' whispered Tucker, a bit quieter this time. Lucas let out a snigger.

'What you muttering about, Tucker?' asked Flymo, getting closer.

'Nothing. I'm just looking for a blank tape, that's all.' He pulled himself out of the cupboard while Larks gave his mate a nudge to remind him to keep quiet.

'What you two doing anyway?' Flymo demanded again.

'We're going to make a film,' announced Tucker which earned him a glare from Lucas. Why couldn't he keep his mouth shut?

Flymo laughed. 'What of? Scoffing cakes? Falling asleep? Or is it some stupid car thing?'

'We're entering a cooking competition,' said Tucker.

'You can't cook.'

Tucker pointed at his best friend. 'He's going to teach me.'

'What, Lentil Lucas?' Flymo turned his angry gaze to Larks. 'What I don't get is how someone who eats nothing but vegetables can get fat. I mean, seriously, how many carrots does it take?'

Lucas's hand went up, defensively, to the badge that he always wore that said: *Animals are my friends. I don't eat my friends!*

'What competition is it?' Flymo barked.

Larks glared meaningfully at Tucker again, but he blurted out, 'It was on *Dinners to Die For*. Two winners get to cook at Mouthful Mansions and then go to Rome to train as real chefs.'

'That programme is rubbish. Proper weirdo chefs those three are. They won't like your veggie stuff. That tall skinny one, whatshisname, only eats chicken.'

'How do you know if you never watch it?' Lucas accused.

'Shut it, Larks.' Flymo shook a fist. Lucas backed off.

'What *are* we going to make?' asked Tucker, turning to his friend.

'Mushroom Mayhem,' Lucas answered. This was a brilliant idea. None of the other entries would get their ingredients from foraging. Larks could see Tucker liked it, but Flymo scoffed. 'You'll have to cook with meat if you want to be a real chef,' he snapped.

'And that's where you are wrong,' Lucas said,

touching his badge again, 'I'm going to be famous for my vegetarian dishes.'

'Pair of losers,' said Flymo shaking his head and starting to walk away. 'You've got no chance.'

'Phew!' said Tucker, once he was sure Flymo had gone. 'We better make this film good, Larks, we seriously have to get out of here and prove Flymo wrong.'

Chapter Three

Competition Entry

It took the boys ages, two whole days, to get it right, but when they'd finished, it was brilliant.

The film started in the grounds of Brocken House. Lucas was quite small in the screen at first, but the more he talked, the closer Tucker zoomed in until his face filled the screen.

'Hello, fellow chefs!' he said. 'My name is Lucas Larks, which I used to think was a rubbish name, but now I think it's a good name for a celebrity chef. If you're going to be a famous chef, you need a name that stands out.'

He did quite a lot of talking, because he had to explain things.

'And I'm Brian Tucker, which is an awesome

celebrity name,' said Tucker from behind the camera, and he turned it round so he could grin into it. It went a bit wobbly whilst he put it back on his shoulder.

'You might be wondering why we're not in the kitchen,' Lucas said. 'We're outside because some of the best ingredients don't come from shops, they come from the world around us.'

At this, Lucas opened his arms and Tucker panned the camera round to show all the trees and garden.

'Take our home, Brocken House. An old place for boys like us who don't have any family to take care of them, built in the woods. Looks like you couldn't find any food here, doesn't it? But we're going to take you foraging and then show you how to cook up what we find into something scrummy. Come on.'

Lucas ran off, all excited, and the next shot was when he picked the first of the mushrooms. He knew where to find them, but the boys made it look like they were a new discovery, just like they do on those adventure programmes. That was Tucker's idea.

'Look at these massive field mushrooms!' Lucas was panting a bit from running. You could hear Tucker breathing hard too; that camcorder wasn't light.

'I'm going to pick four of them really close to the ground. I love mushrooms! You can use them in tonnes of different ways. Scientists find more about them every day. Did you know mushrooms are used for medicine? They're brilliant.'

Lucas might've gone on a bit, but everyone had their food thing; FB liked cheese, Miss Downs liked corn-on-the cob (especially if you did it on the BBQ),

Larks liked mushrooms and Tucker liked…everything.

Lucas picked the mushrooms and Tucker zoomed in on them to see their chocolate-rippled bellies. Larks ran off again like a commando. You could hear Tucker tut before he took off after him, bouncing the camera around.

'More wild mushrooms, lots of different sorts,' he said. 'These ones are called fairy ring and they have a soft flavour. I'll pick a few of these, but what we really want is this,' and he pointed to the beefsteak mushroom jutting out of the tree like a tongue. Carefully Lucas took his penknife and cut it cleanly from the bark. He gently placed all the mushrooms in the newspaper bundle he was carrying and put it inside one of his many jacket pockets and then took off running again to where he knew he would find the next ingredient.

'This little white flower is wild garlic. You can eat everything on the plant, but it's the bulb we need.' Lucas dug out the bulb and trimmed it down with his penknife. 'I'm going to take the leaves too, to flavour the milk. Tucker and me have been foraging for a while now, but if you want to have a go you'll need to use a book, or look it up on the internet, to show you which plants are safe – like this one.' He showed the shaved garlic bulb to the camera. 'Right, we just need a couple of ingredients from the veggie patch now and then it's off to the kitchen to get cooking.'

To keep the film snappy they just cut to the kitchen. They had timed it so Cook wasn't about. Miss Downs and Mrs Corneal liked Lucas to cook, but sometimes he had to be a bit sneaky. His badge was not just for decoration, and what Flymo said about picking locks wasn't far off the truth.

All the ingredients were neatly laid out on the worktop in little bowls and the camera was perched up high, filming from above. The boys had practiced to make it seem they cooked together regularly.

'We call this recipe "Mushroom Mayhem"!' Tucker explained to the camera. 'There's no money in the place we live so we're using old French bread. This is a bit hard,' he whacked the loaf against the worktop and it ricocheted off, 'as it was for yesterday's breakfast, but we can turn this into something tasty.'

He sounded pretty convincing, and slowly sliced the bread, his tongue poking out in concentration. Lucas explained how the beefsteak mushroom had to be soaked in milk to take out the bitterness. Tucker fried the chopped mushrooms and garlic in butter just like he'd been shown and Lucas seasoned the mix with thyme. There was enough for a few portions, which Lucas plated up to look amazing. They gobbled some up.

'Scrummy,' Tucker said between yummy noises and they both grinned up at the camera, with their thumbs up. They wanted to end it there, but Tucker had to lean up to switch it off so the last thing you saw was his wobbly belly.

The boys watched that tape over and over, and then Miss Downs helped them package it off properly. They'd done it – they'd entered the competition. Now came the wait.

Chapter Four
The Letter

It was the end of the holidays when little Stanley Jones, the new kid, brought a letter addressed to Lucas Larks and Brian Tucker to the dorm room.

'Here.' Stanley passed the letter up to Tucker who, like Larks, had a top bunk because he'd been at Brocken House.

Tucker looked at the letter, then threw it across at Larks like it was burning his fingers. 'You open it,' he said. 'I can't do it.'

Lucas moved FB out of the way then ripped open the envelope. He started to read it out loud to Tucker, but he was reading it to Stanley too, and all the others who had started to gather like ants do when your ice lolly melts on the ground.

'Dear Mr Larks and Mr Tucker,

Phil Feathers, Larissa Partum-Nokes and I were very impressed by the quality of your video entry and the dish that you prepared together. You both stood out for all of us as the clear winners, despite the enormous number of entries we received. We would therefore like to invite you both to Mouthful Mansions for a whole weekend of cooking with us.'

'You're having a laugh,' said Tucker. 'Let me look at that.'

He reached across, taking the letter back, his eyes started moving double time across the paper.

'Read it out, then,' Lucas protested.

'If we continue to be impressed with your cooking (as I'm sure we will be) then it will be straight off to Culinary School in Rome.

I will make all the arrangements with your guardians and send a car to collect you. Make sure you bring everything you own and say all your goodbyes. A new life awaits you both!

Congratulations on your win and I look forward to meeting you.

Best wishes,
Leonardo De'Largio'

Tucker stopped and gawped at Lucas. 'No way,' he said and his eyes were all wide, 'that is totally awesome; we only went and won it, Larks!'

He shook the letter about like a flag to the audience, launched himself off his bunk and landed with a massive thud. He started jumping up and down on the spot, squealing like a piglet.

'You jammy gits,' said Flymo. 'Give me that.'

The bigger boy tried to swipe the letter out of Tucker's hand. Tucker was too quick for Flymo, he dodged him and carried on jumping up and down like a Mexican bean.

Lucas wanted to scream and shout and jump about too, but instead he just sat there, as if he was glued to his bunk. He could feel tingles spreading up from his toes to his head and wanted them to keep going until it all exploded out of the top, like popcorn. He could feel a grin spreading across his face and his whole body trembling.

'We got to show Miss Downs,' Tucker said, and he was already running to the door of the dorm room, followed by all the other jealous boys. 'We won it Larks!' Tucker called over his shoulder, 'We're getting out of here.'

Lucas floated from his bunk and followed the trail of boys to Miss Downs's room on the ground floor. He couldn't feel the stairs or the floor underneath him; it was like he was drifting along on a cloud. Stanley took hold of Lucas's hand and gently weaved him through the crowd of kids, until he was stood at the front, next to Tucker, who banged on Miss Down's door.

'Miss Downs, you got to come out and read this!' Tucker's voice sounded weird, like he was underwater.

A groan came from inside Miss Downs's room.

'Now you're for it,' said Flymo, 'She hates getting

up on a Saturday, she's going to go mental.' He grinned a bit at the other kids but nothing could spoil Lucas's floating feeling.

Finally the door opened and a woman, who looked a bit like Miss Downs but sort of crinkled, like a piece of toast waiting to be buttered, peered out. Tucker waved the letter at her.

'This had better be good,' she snapped, looking between the faces of the crowd gathered outside her door.

'Just read it,' said Tucker.

Miss Downs snatched the letter and retreated into her room closing the door behind her.

'Told you,' said Flymo, 'There's no way a couple of losers like you are going to Mouthful Mansions. That letter has to be a mistake.'

'It looked real,' said a little voice.

Flymo turned around to see Stanley looking up at him.

'And what would you know, bug?' snarled Flymo.

'I've seen proper letters, official ones and that's what they look like.'

Flymo's jaw clenched and Lucas started to feel worried for little Stanley's health, but then there was an excited squeal from inside Miss Downs's room. The door opened and out she flew in her blue pyjamas and pulled Lucas and Tucker into a hug.

'We've got to show Mrs Corneal,' she said into the tops of their heads. It was then that Lucas knew it was real, that they were leaving Brocken House, that they'd really won.

Chapter Five

Cooking Lessons and Limousines

After a couple of days, everyone lost interest and the party feeling fizzled out, like a soufflé going flat. Lucas used the time they had left at Brocken House to try and teach Tucker to cook.

'We'll just start with some basics.' Larks laid out some everyday cooking utensils on the worktop.

'I don't need basics, I'm well over all that,' said Tucker, shaking his head.

'All right, not basics then, call it a refresher for me. Okay. To start, what's that for?' he asked him, pointing at the whisk.

'It's a fluffer, for like fluffing up stuff to make it dead fluffy.' Tucker was trying to look wise.

'It's a whisk,' Lucas explained. 'You use it for sauces and for making egg white stiff, or for whipping cream. Sometimes we need to get air into the ingredients, that's when we use a whisk.'

'If you know, why ask me?'

'Because you need to know what I do.'

Tucker stifled a yawn and started staring about the kitchen.

'What about this?' Lucas asked ignoring him and pointing at the potato masher.

'Easy, a squisher thingamy, for squashing stuff so it's all squishy.'

FB wound round Lucas's legs and looked up at him in sympathy. 'Almost. It mashes things. We use it for potato, but you can mash tonnes of stuff like swede and carrot, or parsnip.'

'Parsnip? You mean those big purple things?'

'No,' Lucas said, trying to keep his cool, 'they're aubergines.' He rubbed this face. 'Let's just get to grips with all the equipment and what it's for and then I'll go through ingredients, yeah?'

'Right Chef, whatever you say, but…' he glanced at his watch, 'Can we be quick, because Crankshaft is on in like ten minutes, and I can't miss this week, because…'

'Tucker,' Larks said, interrupting him, 'If you can't cook before we go they're going to know and then they might throw us both out before we've even begun.'

He grinned. 'You worry too much my friend. We

won it. They can't change things now. We're going to Rome, for sure.'

That was how things went, it was hopeless. The truth was Tucker couldn't cook, not at all. Lucas worried the celebrity chefs would smell a rat and the whole thing would be called off before they got anywhere near Italy.

One Saturday morning a white stretch limousine arrived to collect the boys. Tucker didn't have to say anything; his mouth was so round it was like the hole inside a donut.

Everyone at Brocken House came out to see them off, even Flymo. The boys went round giving high-fives, like they were film stars. Even Mrs Corneal slapped Lucas's hand. It was brilliant.

'Are you really going?' Stanley asked Larks.

'Yeah, why?'

'It's just if you go, then we're going to have to eat the yucky stuff that Cook makes.'

Lucas laughed. 'You'll survive,' he said, made up that they liked his cooking.

The special goodbye was for Miss Downs. 'I can't find FB anywhere,' Lucas said quietly into her ear when he gave her a hug.

'Don't worry,' she whispered back, 'I'll slip him some cheese later.'

'What am I going to do with Tucker?' he asked her. Together they watched Tucker, who was doing his rubbish break dance, ripple body thing to show off in front of the other kids.

Miss Downs lent over and whispered again.

'You do the cooking, just let Tucker do the talking, everything will be fine.'

She smiled and then said, 'I'm so proud of you Lucas Larks. You're destined for great things you know?'

'Thanks, Miss Downs.' Lucas looked away and found he had to swallow down a hard lump in his throat.

The driver wore a smart uniform and matching hat. He took their bags and put them in the boot (which seemed ridiculously tiny compared to the length of the car) then he opened the door and tipped his hat. Lucas grinned at Tucker and they scrambled onto the back seat. It smelt like furniture polish. Lucas pushed the window button on the door and leaned out to wave. Tucker did the same on the other side. The driver began to pull away and the boys shouted out, 'Goodbye!' at all the waving hands.

'Flymo,' shouted Tucker, '*You're* the loser.'

Tucker made the L shape on his forehead with his fingers. Lucas laughed, and leant out of his window to do the same. Flymo was running after the limo, waving his fist. The boys laughed into the wind as Brocken House and Flymo disappeared.

Chapter Six

Arriving at Mouthful Mansions

The car went along smoothly, as if it was hovering just above the road. Lucas was doing that flicking thing with his eyes; looking between outside and his own grinning reflection in the window.

'I keep thinking about meeting the celebrity chefs for real,' said Tucker.

'I know! Do you reckon they'll be the same as on the telly?'

Tucker looked thoughtful. 'They'll be thinner. Telly makes you fat and they'll be wearing something normal.'

'What's that stuff Lady Poshnosh wears again? Sounds like swede?'

'Tweed,' said Tucker.

'Yeah, tweed.'

'You won't be able to call her Lady Poshnosh, or Lady P to her face though Larks, better get used to saying Larissa Partnum-Nokes.'

'That's way too hard. At least Feathers is part of his name. We can just call them all Chef anyway, that's what people do on TV.'

There was a pause, before Tucker said, 'I reckon they'll look weird in jeans and a T-shirt.'

Lucas nodded, wondering if they made jeans big enough for Leonardo.

They started fiddling with everything in the car and Tucker gave a running commentary of its spec: 'luxury sedan, V8 engine, chrome wheels…' that kind of thing.

Lucas opened the sunroof, back and forth and checked all the little compartments. Tucker flicked through the radio then the TV stations. The boys were just getting into a cartoon about a crazy spaceship out of control when the car drove over something, making them jump in their seats. Lucas sat up and peered out of the window. They were driving over what looked like a drawbridge.

Tucker was pressed up against his own window too. 'Wicked,' he said, 'It's got proper chains and everything. That must be a moat.'

'I thought moats went round the bottom of castles, that has to be a river.'

On both sides of the gravelled road were tall, tidy trees and grass mowed into stripes. The driver pulled up in a big courtyard next to a fountain of spitting mermaids. Tucker's mouth hung open and his tongue flopped out, like a dog.

The engine stopped and the boys heard the driver get out and his feet crunching on the gravel. Tucker slid along the seat in one skilled move until he crashed into his friend. The driver opened the door and the smell of freshly cut grass came flooding in. Tucker pushed Larks out of the car. Lucas stumbled a bit getting his balance, then it was their turn to walk over the stones, only trainers didn't sound quite as crunchy as the driver's shiny shoes.

'Hey,' said Tucker, staring up at Mouthful Mansions, 'it's like that castle we went to with school, remember? When we were learning about the Romans?'

'You mean the Tudors?'

'Same thing… I wonder if it's got rooms that are blocked off with red ropes with hooks on the end.'

'Check the lawns to see if it says, "Keep off the grass" in red letters.'

They laughed, making the driver turn to peer at them from underneath the brim of his hat, but he didn't say anything.

Lucas's legs shook as they walked up the big curved stone steps. The driver pulled on a golden bell cord. Lucas was glad the driver was there in case he fainted and needed catching; he didn't trust Tucker not to drop him.

It was Leonardo that opened the door. He was even bigger than on *Dinners to Die For*. He was like a giant! *So much for Tucker's theory*, Lucas thought.

'Hello Lucas Larks, and hello Brian Tucker,' he said. His Italian accent was louder in real life. He smiled, showing off his straight teeth. They were as white as the stripe in his hair. Leonardo stuck out a huge hand. It jutted fully out of his body but only reached as far as his belly. Lucas put out his own hand and Leonardo's huge paw swallowed it up. He pumped the boy's arm up and down.

'Hi,' Lucas squeaked.

He let go and did the same to Tucker who babbled, 'Hi Mr De'Largio, you look just like you do on the telly.' And grinned at him.

'Call me Leonardo,' he boomed.

'Okay, if you say so, then Leonardo it is. I'm Tucker and he's Larks.' Tucker gestured at his friend with his thumb.

'Come in, come in,' Leonardo said, wobbling to the side to let them both into Mouthful Mansions. 'Don't worry about bags. Come in and meet us. We are keen for you to come and here you are arriving.'

Lucas felt weird being at Mouthful Mansions looking at his all time hero. He had seen him so many times on the TV; it was almost as though he knew him already.

The chef turned his huge body around by kind of rocking it from side to side and wobbled back inside the mansion. Tucker was right beside him, as if Leonardo was an old friend he'd known for years. Lucas followed but he wasn't walking; it was more of an excited jiggle from one foot to the other. He kept thinking: *we're at Mouthful Mansions*! He could almost hear the theme tune to *Dinners to Die For* coming out of the walls.

There was a trace of delicious home-baked bread in the air and Lucas went from wanting to sniff it in, to wanting to touch everything and then back to staring at Leonardo who was listing dangerously from side to side like a ferry in rough seas.

'We go this way. You know everybody from television. You like the show?'

'Yeah!' the boys said together.

'It's the best thing on telly,' Lucas said, nodding fast. 'I don't cook meat, but most of the dishes you do I can make veggie.'

Leonardo stopped rocking. 'No meat, not ever?' He was staring right at Lucas who had to stop himself jumping up to touch the white stripe in his hero's hair. 'How can anyone not eat meat?' he asked.

Lucas pointed at his badge. 'I was wearing it in our film and we cooked a vegetarian dish? I thought it was one of the reasons we'd won?'

'And you?' he asked Tucker, ignoring what Lucas had said, 'You no cook meat?'

'Well I...' Tucker looked at his friend who was shaking his head vigorously, 'I can, if that's what you mean, but I prefer not to, meat is so, well... dead.'

'But you eat it, no?'

'Yeah, I eat it! I eat everything and anything.' Tucker rubbed at his belly.

'Just like me,' said Leonardo. He smiled and carried on with his wobbly walk.

Leonardo reached double doors and pushed them both open at once. There was suddenly lots of sunlight and the amazing smell of bread got stronger.

The new room was big with a really long table in the middle surrounded by high backed, matching chairs. An enormous golden throne sat at the head of the far end. It looked big enough for a banquet. Around the throne sat the other two celebrity chefs, Larissa Partnum-Nokes and Phil Feathers. There was another man with them wearing a chef's hat. Papers were spread out across the table between them. As they came in the chefs looked up from their papers. Leonardo wobbled his way along the far side of the table and the boys hopped excitedly along on either side of him.

'Lookie who has arrived,' Leonardo boomed across the room, 'our budding chefs!'

Lady P and Feathers pushed their chairs back and came towards them. Chef Hat stayed sitting and started pulling all the papers towards him.

Lady P marched forwards, nose high in the air, like a dog sniffing them out. She was wearing her full tweed outfit. She used her short arms to pump the air as she marched on stumpy legs. Lucas could hear the rustling of the rough material on her sleeves against her thick waist. Her hands were curled up into fists. She wore so many gold rings they all bunched together to look like knuckle-dusters.

By contrast, ambling behind her like a good-natured giant, came Feathers. Lanky and thin, he sort of tumbled along. His strides were enormous but he made no noise at all. His arms kind of bowed out all spindly from his skinny sides. He reminded Lucas of those daddy-long-legs that get stuck in the bath. His nose was huge! His face was all nose, with just a tiny pulled-in mouth hidden under its shadow that made Larks think of FB's bum. He had stretched-out skin above thin eyebrows and a tiny patch of hair up top. His head was shaped like an egg.

Lady P reached them first. She looked Lucas up and down, did the same to Tucker, then thrust out one of her ringed hands for Lucas to shake, which he did. She shook the whole of him so hard his teeth rattled inside his head.

'Excellent work, boy,' she said. 'Glad to see you have some meat on your bones, sign of good stock and shows you like your food eh?'

She gave Lucas a funny, squinty kind of wink.

'Thank you,' Lucas muttered, not quite sure how to respond.

She nodded her head three times in quick little jerks, let go of his hand and marched over to Tucker to do the same. Lucas's hand felt a bit bruised but he needn't have worried, as Feathers's grasp was as weak as a baby's.

'Welcome and congratulations, a worthy winner I think,' he said.

He was smiling, at least Lucas thought he was, it was hard to tell what his mouth was doing under that huge nose. He had little beady eyes, sunk back into his head that flicked over Lucas and then Tucker.

'Did you ask the boys, Leonardo?' Feathers was looking up at the Big Man.

'Ah yes, thanks for remind.' Leonardo turned to Tucker and Larks. 'Have you phone or camera?' he asked them.

'Listen Leonardo,' started Tucker, 'do you think we would've sent that massive ancient video tape in for our competition entry if we had a phone or a camera?'

Leonardo laughed, it boomed through the room. The other two joined in a bit.

'We have to check,' muttered Feathers. 'We are, as you know, well-known celebrities, but we like to keep our home life private.'

'Makes sense,' Tucker said. 'You don't want us sneaking about taking pictures of you and sending them to our mates.'

'Precisely boy, you've hit the nail on the head there.' Lady P nodded her head sharply.

'Well you don't need to worry; we've never had a phone, Brocken House doesn't have the money. Once we get to Italy though eh, Larks?'

Leonardo laughed again. 'A boy with spirit, let's just hope you cook as good as you talk, no?'

Lucas glanced nervously at Tucker, but he was grinning up at the Big Man.

'Come and meet our… meet Christo,' Leonardo said, breaking the moment and he made a sweeping gesture with his arm as if he was opening a heavy curtain. He began making his way towards the end of the table. Lucas thought the other chefs might walk behind him – he was the Head Chef after all – but Lady P marched forwards as if leading her army into battle and Feathers quickly floated his way back to his seat way before Leonardo reached the top of the table.

Lucas was still sort of hopping from one side to another and staring about, worried that if he blinked for too long it would all be gone and they'd be back at Brocken House.

'Christo is an old friend,' explained Leonardo, 'back from when we wore little grey school shorts in Italy.'

The man Leonardo called Christo got up off his chair, but he was barely any taller than when he was sitting. He was bent in a long curve like a banana. He was so curled that he had to twist his head up and to the side in order to see, like potted herbs straining towards the light. He was dressed in spotless chef whites and the hat miraculously stayed planted to the top of his head. The skin on his face and hands looked grey, as if he never saw any sunshine, and his fingers were long and gnarled, with horrible knobbly knuckles sticking up and out. He made no effort to shake Lucas's hand, leaving it hanging.

Tucker didn't offer his hand. Christo looked Larks up and down with a disapproving sneer then did the same to Tucker. He was creepy.

'Christo understands most English, but he speaks only tiny itsy little bit,' said Leonardo, squishing his two fat fingers together.

Lucas looked away from Christo. He was spoiling things. Looking at him was like realising you'd put too much salt in your porridge. Leonardo launched into a long stream of quick Italian, which sounded like piano notes. Christo replied with a few grunted out words then he picked up the papers that were now tidied into a blue file labelled EATS 23. Christo tucked the file under his arm and shuffled off to the far end of the room, head down, muttering to himself. They both hoped they wouldn't be seeing much of him over the weekend.

Chapter Seven

Postcards

Leonardo gave a lumbering tour of some of Mouthful Mansions. He finished by showing their next-door bedrooms. Both had a huge four-poster bed and a separate bathroom. He left the boys to settle in, except he called it, 'settly inside'.

The second Leonardo shut the door Lucas jumped backwards onto the bed. After a minute or two Tucker came barging in.

'Whatever mate, this is just ridiculous,' he said and slumped down next to Lucas. They grinned at one another then Tucker asked, 'How much do you reckon this bed's worth?'

Without thinking Lucas answered, 'Like a million or something.'

Thankfully, Tucker let it go. 'Did you check out the nose?'

'Did I? I think even the neighbours could check it out and they are, like, at least five miles from here.'

They laughed. Tucker jumped off the bed and started doing his Feather's impression. 'Where's the chicken, Leonardo?' he squawked whilst strutting around the room with his elbows flapping. 'This really isn't as good as my dish last week.'

Lucas cracked up even more. 'He has a beak for a nose, his surname is Feathers and what does he love to eat?'

'Chicken,' they said in unison and fell back on the bed laughing.

'And the costumes are real!' said Tucker. 'I mean they actually wear that stuff in real life.'

'I know, what's with that? They must get so hot, especially when they're cooking.' Then Lucas turned a bit more serious. 'Listen, about the cooking thing, Tucker. We have to pretend that you can do it.'

Tucker didn't say anything.

'I reckon they're going to be testing us. We can't mess up, otherwise there'll be no Rome and we'll be back at Brocken House, no passing Go, no collecting two hundred quid.'

'I hear you, my friend,' said Tucker. 'The last thing we want is to slink back to Brocken House with our tails between our legs and have to face a smug Flymo.'

'Exactly.'

'We got this far as a team Larks, we can get to Rome, I know we can. I'll just follow your lead.'

They lay back on the bed for a bit. Lucas was glad that Tucker was seeing things his way. They only needed to pretend he could cook for the weekend and then they'd be in Rome. Lucas had never been on an aeroplane before, it was going to be amazing. Once they were there he wouldn't have to teach Tucker anymore, it would be down to the Italian chefs to take over and good luck to them. They were quiet for a bit, letting the craziness of everything settle like a simmering sauce.

'That Christo's a bit creepy isn't he?' Lucas finally said.

'A bit? He's freaked me right out,' said Tucker.

'He's got to be a chef, wearing all that stuff, but why do they need another chef?'

'How should I know?'

It was quiet, so much quieter than Brocken House. There was never any peace there.

'Hey, you know what we should do?' said Tucker at last, 'We should write a postcard to Miss Downs.'

'How?'

'With these.' Tucker reached into his hooded top, into the secret inside pocket and pulled out a handful of postcards, a pen, and a book of stamps.

'Where did you…?'

Tucker grinned. 'Miss Downs gave them to me before we left. No phone, no problem.'

'She never said that.'

'Well, no. So, come on, you're better at words than me, what shall we say?'

'Oh – says the boy whose not stopped talking since the day I met him.'

'Talking isn't writing though is it? Come on Larks.'

Lucas sighed and sat up next to him. Tucker was writing the post card against his bent up knees.

'Just write: arrived safe, it's brilliant, can't wait to fly to Rome, tell Flymo to take a running jump off the nearest cliff.'

Tucker didn't say anything for a while. He just sat and chewed the end of his pen and stared about him. It was like being back at school sitting next to him, so Lucas left him to it, got up and almost tripped over his bag which was lying open, with clothes falling out.

'Hey, all my stuff is everywhere,' Lucas complained, shoving it back. 'And it's all messed up. Have you been through my bag?'

'Why would I want to look at your knickers?'

'I don't know – maybe you want to borrow them?'

Tucker pulled a face at Lucas who went over to the window. He watched the water from the mermaids arc through the air, then counted the trees that led off down the drive to the river, twelve on each side. He stretched his neck round wondering how far the river went.

'We should go exploring,' he said. 'I bet there's tonnes of good foraging out the back. Funny isn't it, how different the front and the back are? Do you think they only keep the front all neat for the TV?'

'Probably.'

'Where are the gardeners?'

'Larks, it's a Saturday, give them a break.'

'Oh, yeah. Hey, we only have to cook tomorrow

probably then we'll be off to Rome on Monday. We can blag it for one day surely?'

'I told you my friend, it'll be a breeze.'

Lucas's tummy did a little excited flip. He tried to open the window, but it was locked shut. 'Is your window locked too?' he asked.

'What? Not tried. Better not be, you know I hate feeling shut in. Right, what do you think to this: Dear Miss Downs. We're here at Mouthful Mansions, it's massive! Lady P is dressed ready to go hunting, but no sign of any horse. Feather's nose is almost as big as Leonardo's bum. Wish you were here. Love L and T. Kiss. Kiss.'

'You can't write that, what if they read it?'

Tucker shrugged, 'Serves them right for being nosey.'

Lucas laughed and walked back to the bed to sit next to his friend. 'Can you believe we're really here?'

'No. It's completely mental.'

'I keep thinking someone's going to just pop up and say "only joking, here are the real winners, off you go". Do you know what I mean?'

'Totally.'

They sat side by side on the edge of the bed swinging their legs.

'Do you reckon it's been long enough?' Lucas asked.

Tucker checked his watch. 'Yeah, let's go down.' He tucked the spare postcards, stamps and pen back in his hoodie pocket and they started to race each other back.

The celebrity chefs were huddled together around

the breakfast bar and turned in surprise as the boys both skidded to a halt about where Lucas guessed one of the big TV cameras should be. He felt suddenly shy and babyish. Tucker walked up in a sensible more grown-up way as if they'd never been racing at all. He waved Miss Down's postcard at Leonardo.

'I have a postcard,' he said. 'It's for our, well, one of the care workers at Brocken House. Where can I post it?'

Feathers glanced over at Leonardo but the Big Man put one of his massive mitts in the air, which stopped the other chef from saying whatever he was going to say.

'Give to me and I will make sure it posted today, okay?' Leonardo said to Tucker.

Lucas looked nervously at Tucker, but he handed the postcard over without flinching. Leonardo took the postcard and slotted into an inside pocket of his jacket, behind his mobile phone which was just poking out the top. Lucas hoped he wouldn't read it.

'You say it's to someone at orphanage?' Leonardo asked Tucker.

'Yeah,' Tucker said nodding, but not looking right at him. *Go on Tucker*, Lucas thought, *bring him up to date*. 'Only...' added Tucker after a moment, 'we call it a care home, not an orphanage.'

'Why?' Leonardo asked him.

Tucker glanced at Lucas who nodded back, telling him to carry on.

'Some, well most, of the kids who live there still have family and stuff, so they're not really orphans.'

Lucas felt squidgy inside, like uncooked pizza dough, listening to Tucker talk about Brocken House.

Both of them had wanted to get away, but it was the only proper home they'd ever known. It was strange to think they'd have to make a new life in a whole new country.

'But you, you don't have any family do you?' Lucas noticed that it was not only Leonardo who was staring hard at Tucker as he asked this, all the chefs were. Even Christo had stopped whatever he was doing in the kitchen and was watching Tucker. It was like they were testing him.

'No,' Tucker said and his voice was tiny. He was looking at his feet. 'I don't know where my family is, or if I ever had any.'

Lucas felt sad then, really bad for his friend.

'And you?' Leonardo said, swinging his huge body round so that he was looking at Lucas instead.

Lucas shook his head and just like Tucker, didn't look at the enormous chef, or any of the others who he could feel were starting at him. Even Tucker didn't know Lucas's story; there was no way he would blurt it out now. Some kids at Brocken House couldn't wait to tell anybody everything, but most, like Larks and Tucker, kept quiet. Talking about it never changed anything; it was better to forget.

What the boys said seemed to ease things, because the chefs all stopped staring at them. It was like the big spot light had gone away and Lucas let out a breath.

'Well, don't worry,' said Leonardo, his voice all bright again. 'The school in Italy will soon become your family – that is if we like your food.'

Lucas glanced nervously over at Tucker but he was still looking at the floor.

Chapter Eight

Cooking at Mouthful Mansions

The studio kitchen cupboards were full to bursting, loads more food than at Brocken House. The chefs had left the boys to spend a bit of time getting used to where things were kept and what was what. Tucker joined in, the horrible moment from earlier all forgotten.

The kitchen was exactly like on the TV show, with brilliant white surfaces and cupboards that opened with the tiniest touch of a finger. Lucas kept pushing them and clapping his hands as he watched all the magical ingredients appear, then shutting them again. Tucker called him a 'kitchen geek'. He kept pulling things out and asking what they were.

There was a ginormous fridge freezer, big enough to walk into, and a drawer with a triple row of spices and herbs. There were stewing pots, a slow cooker, a juicer, two sinks, masses of worktop space, a food processor, two triple ovens with double hobs and hot plates. Three different drawers held everything from the sharpest, smallest paring knives, to enormous plastic ladles.

The kitchen was laid out in an L-shape with a long breakfast bar style worktop. It was open so that the film crew could manoeuvre around easily and get close-up shots of the bits they needed for the show. There were tiny cameras embedded in the walls, but their lights were off. High bar stools clustered around the end of the breakfast worktop. Lucas could imagine Lady P's stumpy legs kicking out, too short to reach the ground.

'What are we going to cook?' Tucker asked.

'Well, they said we need three courses, just like in *Dinners to Die For* so I reckon we just have a good look to see what they've got.'

The door behind swung open and in walked Christo with a tray of uncooked rolls. That was why Mouthful Mansions smelt so good. It was amazing Christo could see where he was going.

'What's he doing here?' asked Tucker in his too-loud whisper.

'Shut up,' Lucas whispered back. 'Just go with it.'

Christo started busying himself at the back of the kitchen, chopping up tomatoes and fresh herbs. He turned on an oven for his bread.

Lucas went to the fridge, pulling Tucker's sleeve to

stop him gawping at the wizened chef. He opened up the door and together they peered inside.

'What is all this stuff?' Tucker asked, poking at different vegetables.

'These are fava beans,' Lucas said passing them to him. 'These are avocados, this is radish cress, and this is a red onion.' He stacked them all in Tucker's arms.

'Right,' said Tucker his face poking up over the cress.

'Do you know what this is?' Lucas asked him.

'Lemon?'

'Excellent. We're going to make salad to start. Put it all on the worktop over there.' Lucas gestured with his head.

When they closed the fridge and stood up they saw Lady P, Leonardo and Feathers walking towards them. The celebrity chefs all clutched notepads and pencils in their hands.

'You start, that's good,' said Leonardo. He waved a hand, 'Carry on.'

Lucas took the couscous out of the cupboard. 'Boil the kettle,' he said out of the side of his mouth to Tucker.' He poured the couscous into a bowl and got the seasoning ready.

'What is that you've got there?' asked Feathers, poking a finger at the ground cumin and chilli flakes mix.

Lucas knew he was testing him, making sure he knew what he was doing. Lucas told him and explained how they were going to mix everything together to make a fava bean salad to start.

'Would it go with chicken do you think?' he asked and Lucas could hear Tucker trying not to laugh.

'Well, I don't eat chicken, but this would make a delicious side dish,' Lucas started to say, but Feathers interrupted him.

'Wait, stop. Did you just say that you don't eat chicken?' he asked, completely amazed.

'I don't eat any meat,' Lucas explained.

'What, never?' asked Lady P, looking just as shocked as Feathers. 'Not even a lovely juicy young rabbit?'

'No,' said Tucker. 'He definitely wouldn't eat a rabbit. Look at his badge.'

Tucker pointed to Lucas's badge and the two chefs squinted to read it.

'The other boy he say yes,' said Leonardo nodding over at Tucker, 'but this one, no meat at all. It is strange, no?'

'Not really that strange,' Lucas said, feeling a bit braver. 'Lots of people are vegetarian.'

'But why?' asked Lady P. 'When there are so many different animals to eat, why wouldn't you just shoot them and eat them?'

Lucas tried not to wince at the thought of innocent animals being shot.

'He's got a theory,' said Tucker, happier to chat about his friend than pretend to cook. 'He likes a good theory does Larks.'

Lucas let Tucker explain and got on with the chopping.

'Go on boy, I'm genuinely interested,' urged Lady P.

Tucker leant up against the breakfast bar. It reminded Lucas of when Miss Downs gossiped with Mrs Corneal. 'Larks will only eat what he could kill and cook himself,' he said.

'Aha,' said Lady P winking at Lucas. 'A fellow hunter, good, good, that's marvellous.'

Tucker sniggered a bit. 'He's definitely no hunter, can't even swat a fly without feeling bad.' He turned to his best mate. 'You could just about catch a fish and gut it and that, couldn't you Larks?'

Lucas nodded.

'But never a pig?' Tucker added.

Lucas grimaced at the horrible thought of it.

'What about a chicken?' asked Feathers. 'Surely you could wring a chicken's neck?'

Lucas shook his head, he was beginning to feel sick, even when he saw Tucker clap a hand over his mouth to stop the giggle pop out.

Leonardo laughed and his chins wobbled. 'One eat meat, one not, I wonder if it make a difference?'

Lucas had no idea what he was talking about but thought he should explain. 'I think it has something to do with how big and clever the animal is,' he said, looking down at the onion he was slicing. 'Like a lobster I could kill, but not just by sticking in a boiling pan of water, that's cruel, but a dolphin… well there's just no way.'

The chefs looked at each other and laughed. Lucas felt himself blushing and looked at Tucker leaning against the breakfast bar; he wasn't laughing at all anymore.

'I'm not saying my theory is one hundred per cent,' Lucas said, a bit quieter than before, 'but at least I've thought about it, which in my head is better than just shoving stuff in your mouth without caring.'

Things went a bit quiet after that. Whilst the beans were cooking Lucas pulled Tucker down into a squat at the vegetable rack behind the breakfast bar.

'We're going to make a ratatouille,' Lucas whispered, hopefully out of earshot. 'It's not very original, but a classic.'

'Mate,' whispered Tucker, 'you can't be cooking no rat after that little speech.'

'Just chop this up in thick slices,' Lucas said handing Tucker the huge vegetable he had just found in the rack. 'This is an aubergine, okay?'

'Aubergine, not parsnip, got it,' he said, and used it to salute with.

Lucas found some brown rice and soaked it in cold water whilst they carried on with the rest of the cooking.

Tucker was properly switched on, which was a relief. Lucas watched him chop up the aubergine. His knife skills were poor, but at least he was listening and remembering. Some of the stuff from training at Brocken House must've sunk in.

Occasionally Christo, Tucker and Lucas danced around the kitchen to avoid one another. Sometimes the smells from Christo's side were delicious enough to make Lucas glance over to see what he was doing. Tucker stared at Christo unashamedly.

The celebrity chefs paused the cooking here and there to ask what a certain ingredient was or to ask what they were planning to do with something they'd chopped up. Lucas came to Tucker's rescue a few times but mostly it was brilliant.

Lucas couldn't think too much about the fact he was cooking for the famous chefs at Mouthful Mansions otherwise he might lose it and ruin the food. He knew that the competition was not yet over, but smiled to himself; things were going well.

Christo finished first which meant Lucas could make the lemon cheesecake without being watched too closely. Christo presented each chef with a starter of fresh tomato soup sprinkled with coriander.

'That smells awesome,' said Tucker, practically drooling into Leonardo's whopper of a serving.

Lucas was pretty hungry too, but was glad that Tucker didn't ask for some – even though he looked like he might climb into the leftovers on the stove.

Christo served up his home-baked bread to go with the soup.

'Do you think we're getting any?' Tucker whispered.

Lucas shrugged, 'The way Leonardo is going for it there might not be any left.'

The boys' giggles stopped short when they saw Christo scowl. He was bringing out his main course. It was a chicken dish, some kind of casserole or stew. It came out of the oven in a huge pot.

The chefs tasted it with lots of sucking, slurping and chomping noises and then made little comments and suggestions.

'The sauce around the chicken today could be

good for EATS, don't you agree, Phil?' said Lady P.

Feathers grimaced and looked sidelong at the boys, back at Lady P, then over to Leonardo who gave him a wink and a smile.

'Write it down for EATS then, Larissa. We don't want to forget when it comes to time.'

The boys shrugged at each other. Lady P asked Christo about the recipe for the chicken dish and made careful notes from his stilted English. He lapsed into Italian so Leonardo started off translating, then took over the writing from Lady P.

Christo could really cook. Bread had to be his thing, just like foraging was Lucas's. All chefs had their own thing.

Christo's dessert was tiramisu. Very difficult to do and it looked near perfect.

Leonardo, however, wasn't impressed. 'Christo, no,' he almost shouted, then fell into an angry stream of Italian.

Christo said nothing but his face froze as Leonardo jabbed a sausage finger at his chest. The other chefs stood without doing or saying anything, they almost looked bored. Tucker and Larks glanced at one another, but neither of them had a clue what was going on.

When Leonardo had finished yelling, Christo turned calmly back and began clearing up the mess that always happens when you get creative with food. The boys were too busy with their own dishes to worry too much about it.

'You might be too full, to eat now,' said Tucker.

'Look at me, boys,' said Leonardo rubbing a huge

mitt round and round on his belly, 'you think I get full all easy?' He grinned at them. 'Bring out your no meat food, lets see it and eat it.'

Nervously, Lucas plated up the bean salad for Leonardo. Tucker watched and tried to do the same for Feathers and Lady P.

'Interesting mix of flavours,' said Feathers, 'I like the crunch of the onion against the delicate taste of the beans.'

Lucas could feel the start of a smile.

'Yes, very agreeable to the palate,' Lady P said with three quick nods of her head. 'Quite different to anything we've had before.'

His smile was getting bigger. He felt a nudge in the ribs and turned to see Tucker grinning at him. They waited, carefully watching Leonardo – what he thought was the most important of all.

'Mm, well done boys. I'm interested in this new cooking,' Leonardo said to the other chefs in between forkfuls. Then he said something amazing, 'Join us boys, eat with us.'

Christo, who was still cleaning up, clanged his pots together angrily but the boys both ignored him. Tucker practically fell on the salad and Lucas plated some up for himself too. They ate standing up from the other side of the worktop.

'Oh my God, Larks, that's so yum!' said Tucker, his mouth full of fava beans.

'Good,' Lucas said and tapped his fork against the plate, like a grownup would do. 'We're happy, aren't we Tucker?'

Tucker took the hint and gathered himself together, 'Ah, yes,' he said and tapped his fork too, 'very happy; good combination of flavours.'

The celebrities seemed pleased, that was obviously the right thing to do.

'You can eat boys, whenever and whatever you like, night or day,' Leonardo said, spreading his arms wide to take in the whole kitchen. 'It's all part of it, tasting you know, don't be shy, feel free. Our food is your food.' Leonardo smiled at them and the boys grinned at each other too, still trying to ignore the grumpy clanging of pans behind.

Feeling more confident, they brought out the ratatouille. They gave smaller portions to Lady P and Feathers, but Leonardo kept waving his hand until a huge mound of food sat steaming in front of him. It was amazing how he could eat and eat and eat.

Tucker and Larks ate too. It was delicious, with just the right amount of spice.

'This could be good for EATS too?' Leonardo was talking to Feathers and dabbing at a bit of sauce on his top chin.

'I'll write it down because that would be ironic wouldn't it, I mean if we ended up using it?' The three of them chuckled together.

Lucas didn't know what they were talking about and Tucker was too busy eating to hear. Larks answered Feathers's questions about the ratatouille, all of which was written down carefully in his notebook, licking at the end of his pencil with a tiny pointed tongue that darted to the side his enormous nose.

They loved the lemon cheesecake. Leonardo ate two big slices with cream. It was Lady P who asked most about it: how many lemons, what was the best brand of cream cheese to use, did they use any rind, and all of that. Just like Feathers, she wrote everything down.

Lucas ate his cheesecake, stealing glances over his shoulder at Christo. He was eating his soup and bread in the corner of the kitchen, scowling at the boys. Lucas looked back at the chefs gobbling up their pudding. If the test for culinary school was to beat Christo then it was in the bag, it had to be.

Chapter Nine
Exploring

Leonardo had said, as the chefs left, that when the boys had finished clearing up they were free to explore Mouthful Mansions.

'Come on,' said Tucker making a run for the front door, having put away the last pot, 'I'll race you to the drawbridge.'

Lucas ran after him and they crunched their way down the driveway and over the bridge. Breathing heavily, the friends peered through the chains over the edge into the murky water far below.

'Do you reckon there's anything living in there?' Larks asked Tucker.

'Doubt it,' he said. 'It stinks. Could you swim it, do you reckon? If you had to?'

'No chance!' Lucas answered. 'Look at the banks, they're well steep, you could never get in and out.'

They stared down into the disgusting sludge.

'Plus… you've only just stopped using armbands,' he joked.

Lucas punched him on the arm. 'You're just as rubbish a swimmer as me.'

'Ow!' He rubbed where he'd been hit.

'The water isn't moving at all. It must be some kind of moat, but it's weird how far away from Mouthful Mansions it is.'

'Yeah. This gateway thing has been built specially to drop the bridge up and down over it,' said Tucker.

The boys walked to the huge twisty metal gates at the end of the drawbridge.

'Locked.' Tucker gestured to the big chain and padlock.

'I wonder what happened to the driver,' Lucas said.

'They must've just hired him. What's that?' Tucker was pointing to a small black box on the other side of the gate. Lucas put his hand through a gap in the wrought iron and pulled out the postcard to Miss Downs that was sticking out of it. He read it.

'You liar,' Lucas said and flicked Tucker with the postcard.

'Well. I wasn't really going to write that was I?'

'No wonder you weren't bothered when Leonardo took it from you.'

Tucker grinned and shrugged at the same time.

'Cool,' Lucas said, putting the postcard back, 'Mouthful Mansions has its own special post box.'

'Yeah,' said Tucker. 'Hey, how long do you think it took Leonardo to wobble all the way down here?' He started rocking his body back and forth.

'Maybe he just got someone to do it for him.'

Tucker stopped rocking. 'Like who?'

Lucas shrugged, 'I don't know, maybe the minions only work Monday to Friday. Anyway, doesn't matter, now we know where the post goes, we can write whenever we want to. Not that we'll be here for very long.'

'Who needs phones when you've got snail mail?'

'Come on, let's see just how far this river, or moat or whatever it is, goes,' Lucas said over his shoulder as he started running back across the drawbridge and into the wild grounds of Mouthful Mansions.

The boys followed the moat until the plants got too thick, then they headed into the woods.

'We should get high up,' Lucas said, 'that way we can see more.'

Tucker looked around for a good tree and started heaving himself up onto its' lower branches. Lucas followed him up. It wasn't too hard, but he had to concentrate on keeping his balance. At the top it was brilliant – you could see for miles.

'Look,' Lucas said, pointing down. 'The moat snakes all the way round the forest. It must be at least five or six miles long.'

'The grounds are massive. We'd better head back towards Mouthful Mansions, or we could get lost out here.'

They didn't make any move to climb down though. It was pretty cool being up there in the sunshine looking at everything. An airplane crossed high overhead making a white trail behind.

'That will be us on Monday,' Lucas said, pointing skyward.

They could see the little road from the Mansion snaking away into a bigger one much further in the distance, patchwork fields and scattered woods, but it was the massive Mouthful Mansions that they stared at. Lucas could tell that they'd seen less than half of it on Leonardo's tour.

'You see that window there, nearest us?' Lucas pointed.

'Yeah?'

'There's someone moving inside. That has to be Leonardo. He's doing something with his hair isn't he? He's a bit far away, I can't tell from here.'

'I bet he's colouring it. That white stripe is not natural, that comes from some packet, I'm telling you.'

Lucas laughed. 'What do you know about hair dye?'

Tucker shrugged. 'What's to know?'

They watched Leonardo move away from sight and Lucas started counting all the windows he could see. 'It really is massive,' he said. 'How many kids could live here do you reckon?'

Tucker shrugged again, 'At least a hundred, but seriously if you had their kind of money wouldn't you live in a massive house with just a couple of your best mates? There's no way I would live with a bunch of kids with no homes unless I had to.'

'I suppose, but it still seems a bit of a waste.'

'Come on.' Tucker was starting to climb down. 'Let's go and check out inside a bit more.'

They fought their way through the thick forest back towards the mansion. Lucas wanted to start foraging but Tucker pulled him away. They ran back up the steps and pushed open the heavy front door. On a whim, the boys turned left at the bottom of the stairs and headed towards the library.

Feathers was nosing his way across the dusty shelves, muttering something to himself. He didn't notice the boys at first. He had a book in his hand that he put back on the shelf, then he walked over to a big wall map and put a pin in it, turned and saw them both.

'Ah, hello boys!' he said. 'Readers are you? Good-oh. Come on in and have a browse.'

'Do you have a cook book section?' asked Tucker, strolling in and starting to scan the books.

'Of course,' said Feathers and showed Tucker to the bottom shelves.

Lucas was drawn to the place where Feathers had replaced the book. It stuck out slightly from the others: *South East Asia's Diminishing Species.* Wondering what that meant, he walked over to the wall map, avoiding Tucker who was sitting down on the ground pulling out cookery books and pretending to read them. Feathers was leaning over him, peering at the pages.

The map was covered with different coloured pins. Almost every country in the world had a pin in it. Some were clustered quite tightly together. Lucas looked at the key to the side, but it made no sense, just a jumble of dates and strange letters.

'What's this for?' he asked Feathers.

'Oh, don't worry about that, boy,' Feathers said. 'Just a personal project if you like. Won't make any sense to you.'

Lucas read the title that was written in capitals at the top of the map. It was underlined in red: *EATS DISCOVERY OF THE WORLD!*

'Well, I'll leave you boys to browse the recipes and get some ideas, perhaps for tomorrow?'

Tucker looked up from his book and nodded. 'Catch you later, Chef P,' he said.

Lucas cringed. 'Chef P?' he said to his friend the moment Feathers was out of earshot. 'I thought you were all for using their proper names?'

Tucker shrugged. 'Chef P and Lady P, easier. Let's take some of these to your room,' he said. 'You can teach me a bit more. Either that, or they'll send me to sleep.'

'You don't need any help getting to sleep Tucker.' Lucas's best friend could and did fall asleep anywhere and everywhere.

He laughed. 'No, getting to sleep is well easy, especially when it's in a million-pound bed at Mouthful Mansions.' Tucker nudged his friend playfully.

Chapter Ten

Sunday at Mouthful Mansions

There was a banging noise coming from outside Lucas's bedroom door. Sleepily, he hauled himself up. Then he remembered where he was, he couldn't miss a moment! He jumped up and opened the door. Christo was framed in the doorway wearing a sparklingly clean, full set of chef whites.

He said nothing, just beckoned with one of his horrible, long fingers. Lucas gestured to his old pyjamas; they had holes in the knees and bagged around the bum. Lucas wondered if he dared to ask Christo for a set of his chef whites, but then thought that he probably wouldn't be able to do the buttons up over his tummy. Besides, they'd get chef whites at culinary school for certain, he thought.

Christo shrugged then pointed to his watch, stretched his hand out fully showing all five fingers, then pointed down to the carpet.

'Are you giving us five minutes to be downstairs?' Lucas asked.

Christo smiled, but it was not friendly. 'Not me, he,' Christo said. Then he turned and walked away surprisingly fast, leaving Tucker standing there in his place.

'He's well creepy,' Tucker said, coming into Lucas's room and closing the door behind him. 'Nobody should be that hunched over, it's not normal.'

'Well', Lucas said, as he quickly got dressed, 'we won't have to worry about Christo because tomorrow, my friend, we will be flying to Italy.'

'Do you reckon we've passed the test then?'

'They loved that food,' Lucas called out of the bathroom, putting toothpaste on his brush, 'I reckon today, we'll be cooking with them.'

Tucker and Larks walked into the kitchen and the delicious smell of warm bread hit them like a wave. All the chefs were gathered around the breakfast bar, just like the day before. Lucas almost waved at them.

'Hello, little chefs,' said Feathers. 'What are you cooking us for breakfast?'

'Really? You want us to cook straight away?' Lucas grinned at Tucker – he knew they loved their cooking.

'Of course,' said Lady P. 'You want to be chefs don't you? Then you must cook. Practice, practice, practice.' She thumped one hand into the palm of the other. 'You don't think I became such a crack shot as a girl by sitting around thinking about shooting those damn rabbits do you? No, boys, I went out there with my gun and bang, bang, bang, I shot the damn things to smithereens.' She mimicked shooting a gun from her shoulder. 'Missed at first, I can tell you; nearly shot the neighbour's cat a couple of times. Stupid thing was brown just like the rabbits. But practice gave me skills, and the family grounds were soon rabbit-free.'

Lucas shuddered at the thought of Lady P shooting rabbits and didn't know what to say. He tried to imagine Lady P as a girl. It wasn't easy. Then he felt a gentle shove from behind and turned to see Leonardo's giant hand pushing him towards the kitchen.

'Go, cook boy, make us something impressive.'

Christo was in his side of the kitchen and Lucas wondered if it was another competition. The boys tried to stay out of his way as they rummaged around and Lucas pulled out any ingredients he fancied.

'I'm going to show off my baking skills,' he whispered to Tucker. 'You can weigh out the ingredients for cinnamon and raisin puffs.'

'Gotcha.'

Tucker amazingly went to the right cupboard and got out the scales and a large mixing bowl. Perhaps Lucas would make a chef out of him yet, he thought.

If it was a competition, however, Christo won. He served three different types of bread rolls, with fresh butter and homemade apricot jam. They looked good and the tiny raisin puffs seemed dry and boring sitting along side them. It didn't stop the three chefs from gobbling them up.

'Two teaspoons of cinnamon and a cup of raisins?' asked Feathers with his pencil poised.

'Yep that's what we did,' Tucker said.

Lucas ate one himself. They were much lighter than ones he'd made before, sweet but not too sweet, but he kept eyeing that bread – that was what he really wanted to eat.

'Splendid stuff, boys,' said Lady P, pushing her dirty plate across towards them. 'Now I'm off for a little vermin hunting.' She tucked her notepad and pencil neatly away in an inside pocket and marched out of the kitchen.

'Don't forget the EATS meeting,' called Feathers after her. Lady P raised a hand in the air but didn't turn round.

Lucas hoped she wasn't really going off to shoot rabbits. He wondered if he would have a chance to cook with the celebrities before they left for Italy.

'You stay here boys, yes?'

They nodded at Leonardo to say that was fine. He was daintily removing the flakes of puff pastry from his lower chins.

'You can eat more,' he said to them. 'Eat with Christo and together you clear away. We get together later for more cooking fun.' He winked.

Lucas looked over his shoulder at Christo who was leering at them. He didn't want to hang out with the mean chef, but when he turned to say something Leonardo and Feathers were already making their way towards the doors.

A set of knobbly knuckles grabbed one of the

raisin puffs, so fast it made Lucas jump. He turned to see Christo biting into the pastry. His beady gaze flicked between Tucker and Larks. Lucas couldn't tell whether he liked the puff or not and wondered why he cared.

'Can we?' Lucas asked him, pointing at the gorgeous smelling rolls.

Christo simply shrugged his skinny shoulders. Larks went to take one, but Tucker's hand got in there first. Lucas broke open the soft white bread, which was still warm, spread on the butter that instantly began to melt, and added a dollop of apricot jam. Wow, it was good! He could've eaten twenty

Christo was watching the boys eat; his head all twisted sideways, his sharp eyes waiting.

'That's unbelievable, how do you do that?' Lucas asked, his mouth still full. Tucker didn't speak; it didn't look like he could.

Christo walked out of the kitchen area and gestured for them to follow him. Lucas brought his plate with him and Tucker added a second roll to his plate. That made Christo smile, just a bit, and this time it was friendlier, more real.

Christo took them out of the far door of the kitchen. It led into a white utility room filled with large white cupboards, washing machines and deep sinks. There was another door at the far end of the room, which Lucas guessed probably led outside. Christo opened one of the cupboards. Inside he had racks of bread, all gently rising. The sweet smell washed over them. Lucas breathed it in then took another bite of the roll. He really had a gift; the bread was the best.

'This here,' Tucker said gesturing to the cupboard, his mouth still full of bread, 'is why this place smells so good.'

Christo smiled a little bigger at this.

They went back out to the breakfast bar stools and sat down. It felt, as they sat there talking about food and sharing each other's breakfasts, that something changed. Christo still looked scary, but Lucas knew that they shared a love of cooking. It stopped him feeling afraid.

They had almost finished clearing up when Leonardo came wobbling back into the kitchen.

'You two go outside and look around for ingredients now,' he said to the boys. 'Christo, you find them something to wrap up what they find, like a newspaper.'

Christo disappeared and reappeared almost immediately with a newspaper.

'Good, good, now go,' said Leonardo and made a shooing movement with his enormous hands.

Lucas took the paper and they followed Christo through the door from the kitchen, Leonardo's words still ringing in his ears. Had the chefs got together and changed their minds about their cooking? Had they guessed about Tucker? Had they lost their chance? Christo opened the side door, which did lead outside. Tucker and Lucas walked through but when Lucas turned to say something, Christo closed the door in his face.

'What was that about do you think?' Larks asked Tucker.

'Dunno. I was starting to think that Christo wasn't so creepy after all. Man, that bread tasted good.'

They started to walk into the overgrown wildness.

'It was horrible when he slammed that door, it was like he was shutting us out of something,' Lucas said.

Tucker shrugged. 'Don't worry about it, Larks.'

Lucas glanced down at the newspaper he was carrying and silently read the headline:

Further Illegal Importation of Exotic and Endangered Animals Into the UK.

There was a picture of an orangutan. It didn't have all the big flaps round its head so Lucas knew it was a female. He didn't want to read any more, he was feeling too sad already, so he folded the paper up and tucked it under his arm.

'Hey what's that noise?' he asked.

The boys stopped moving for a minute and listened to the thrashing and crashing that was coming from ahead. Then they heard the unmistakeable voice of Lady P.

'Come out, my little rabbit friends, come on out.'

Tucker grinned, but Lucas was too worried about the rabbits to smile.

'Do you think she's got a gun?' Lucas whispered.

'Yeah. She's a "crack shot" don't forget.'

They stood listening to her thundering about for a while.

'Come out,' they heard her shout. 'Come out you

stupid rabbits, come and see your Auntie Larissa and her little friend Shaun the Shotgun. Ha!'

'Shaun?' whispered Tucker. 'She's named her gun?'

With all that crashing and shouting she was never going to shoot anything. *Good for the rabbits*, Lucas thought.

'Hey, I've just realised – if Lady P is out here they can't have all been talking about us.'

Tucker sighed. 'How many times have I got to tell you Larks? It's in the bag. Tomorrow you and I are on that plane, my friend.'

Feeling much happier, Lucas ignored Lady P and started scanning for mushrooms. They were everywhere! The boys found loads: blushing woods, penny buns, even a big puff ball, but the best were the tiny black mushrooms that grew in clumps around the base of a huge sycamore tree. Tucker was the one who spotted them.

'Hey, what about these?'

Lucas came over to look. 'These are dead rare,' he said.

'What are they?'

'Darkest Devils they're called.'

Tucker pulled back his hand from them like he'd been stung.

'You're safe,' Lucas said, 'and they're tasty, but don't eat more than one or two.'

'Why?'

'Because, you'll be off to the land of nod, my friend and knowing you, you probably won't wake up for a week.'

Lucas picked quite a few, the ones that grew tallest, and left the others alone. That was the thing with mushrooms; you had to know what you were doing. Some were even deadly. Lucas knew a lot, but there was tonnes of stuff to find out.

It was a nice day, warm and bright and the boys kept finding new plants so ended up getting a bit lost. Eventually they found themselves outside the door they thought took them back into the utility room, but instead of a room with white cupboards and washing machines, there were stone steps leading down into a basement.

'That's not right,' Tucker said, 'I don't like the look of it in there.' He backed out into the daylight again.

'Let's have a proper look.' Lucas pulled the door back wide and the sunlight rushed inside. 'Dungeons,' he said. 'Got to be. Let's go down there.'

'No way,' Tucker said. 'We don't want to get caught snooping about. If Leonardo had wanted us to see what was down there he would have put it in his tour. Come on.'

Lucas shrugged and let the door fall back. They stuck to the wall of the castle and eventually found the right door. Tucker knocked twice with his fist and Leonardo answered. The enormous chef looked down at them, his white stripe catching the sunlight. He stared at both boys hard for a moment and then he looked past them.

'Shoot anything?' he asked over the top of their heads.

Lucas turned to see Lady P thundering out of the bushes. She had sticky weed stuck to her deerstalker and a smudge of mud across her nose. She was using her gun like a walking stick. Lucas wondered if it was loaded and if it might just go off suddenly and lift the hat clean off her head.

'No,' she answered, all sort of huffy. 'I've had to come back for the EATS meeting. Cunning little vermin we've got running around here, Leonardo. But I'll get them, you mark my words.'

She pushed past a bit rudely and Leonardo stepped to the side to let her in.

'Is it safe for the boys?' she asked, and Leonardo nodded making the flesh of his chins wobble lazily about. Tucker gave Larks a look. Wondering what she meant, they followed her inside. Lady P marched off, tweeds rustling, nose in the air.

'Find anything, boys?' asked Leonardo. His voice was softer again and he smiled at them, so they showed him their collection of mushrooms. Lucas didn't tell him about how the Darkest Devils can make you sleepy, and was glad Tucker didn't either, but he didn't know why.

'It's very good,' Leonardo said, and gestured for them to follow him into the kitchen. Christo was there busily putting away groceries that had mysteriously appeared whilst they were outside.

'You help Christo now,' said Leonardo, 'and tell him if any more ingredients you need.'

Tucker went on ahead, but Lucas stopped and looked up at the huge man confused, 'But why would we need more ingredients? Isn't today our last day?'

'Yeah,' said Tucker over his shoulder, 'I thought we were off to the school in Rome tomorrow?'

Leonardo waved an arm the size of a tree trunk dismissively through the air. 'We need more time to, how do you say? Assess you both. It is important that you fit into the school in the right way and that takes a bit more time than we thought. Don't look so worry, you'll not be going back to the orphanage, you can be sure of that.'

Lucas didn't know what to think. He was happy to stay at Mouthful Mansions, but if they were still assessing them did that mean they weren't ready for the school in Italy? Perhaps the celebrities weren't as impressed by his cooking as he thought they were or perhaps they were onto Tucker's little scam.

At that moment Feathers opened the door to the kitchen and peered round, his beak of a nose leading the way. 'We're ready for you, Leonardo.'

'Okay, I come.'

Lucas watched Leonardo waddle his way towards the door as Tucker went into the kitchen. Lucas went back into the utility room and found a space for the bundle of mushrooms to dry out at the bottom of Christo's bread cupboard. He closed the door and went into the famous kitchen to join Christo and Tucker with unpacking the shopping, wondering how they could make sure they got into that school.

Chapter Eleven
Cooking With Christo

The next morning, the chefs were all gathered together around the tasting end of the breakfast bar wearing their usual costumes.

'Shall I wake Tucker?' Lucas asked them when he realised his friend wasn't around.

Leonardo waved a hand through the air, 'Leave him to sleep. He learns good skills in Italy, you no worry. You cook with Christo now.'

This was new; this could help, Lucas thought. He could definitely learn a thing or two from Christo. He wondered if he was still being tested and why it was Christo and not the celebrity chefs themselves that he was being asked to cook with. Perhaps they'd worked out that Tucker and Larks were at different levels? Maybe they wanted to see how well Lucas could cook with other chefs? Lucas had to think and quick. He spotted the over full fruit bowl and gestured to it.

'Breakfast fruit salad?' he suggested to Christo.

Christo nodded and moving like lightning whipped out two large chopping boards and some knives. Before Lucas had moved Christo was already peeling and slicing the fruit. He really worked fast; Lucas tried to copy.

It was brilliant cooking with Christo; he got loads of tips. They sort of helped each other. Christo grated some nutmeg into the lemon juice and sugar mix before drizzling it over the finished salad, but it was Lucas who used the darker, more flavoursome muscovado sugar. It was so much better not having to worry about Tucker doing or saying the wrong thing. The chefs, watching from the other side, thought it was funny how they worked together as a team.

'That's it you two, chop, chop, slice, slice, fine bit of co-ordination I'd say and you don't even need to speak the same language,' said Lady P, using her hand in a slicing motion.

'Language of food,' agreed Feathers, 'that's what they have in common. Look how they're arranging the salad, such a tantalising assortment of colours and tastes.'

'You have new friend then, Christo?' asked Leonardo. 'Don't get too attached, remember?'

Christo's purple knuckles tightened more firmly around his knife when Leonardo said that. Lucas started to wonder if Christo might miss him and Tucker when they left for Italy.

The chefs gobbled up the breakfast and wandered off afterwards, probably to another EATS meeting, whatever that was. Christo and Lucas were left to clean up and start planning the next meals. Sitting with him made Lucas think.

'Do you always do the cooking?' Lucas asked him.

'Cook, clean, I do everything,' he said, in his thick Italian accent, the words pushed out of his mouth like he was spitting out orange pips.

'You must get paid loads,' Lucas said, thinking of the limo.

Christo shook his head, 'He no pay me.'

'They don't pay you? But they're millionaires and they're famous, why wouldn't they pay you?'

He just shrugged. Lucas thought about it. Mouthful Mansions was great and everything but he didn't think he would want to live there forever.

'Why do you stay then?' he asked. 'You're a great chef, you could run your own kitchen if you wanted.'

Christo twisted his head to look up at Lucas and he could see he was wondering whether to tell him something important. He touched his top pocket softly and felt inside with his bony fingers. Tenderly he pulled out an old square photo and passed it to Lucas. The photo was faded but Lucas could make out Leonardo as a round boy of about nine or ten. He had one of his plump arms over the thin shoulders of Christo, the boy next to him and the pair were grinning into the camera. Christo was skinny even then, the beginnings of his hunched back already showing. His thin arms were hanging limply by his side. They were both in school uniform, little grey shorts (just like Leonardo had said), emblazoned shirts and old-fashioned cloth caps on their heads.

'He help me, he protect me.' Christo explained.

'You mean from other boys?' Lucas asked and Christo nodded.

Larks thought about Flymo and little Stanley and understood.

'He's your friend?' Lucas asked, but it wasn't really a question.

'He was good friend to me.' Christo took the photo and put it safely back in his pocket. As he did so, a memory came to Lucas's mind.

'Why did he get angry about the tiramisu?'

Christo dropped his gaze to the ingredients for lunch laid out ready. He picked at the feathery tops of the carrots. 'He like new things. I make that before.'

'But why don't they cook themselves? They all cook on the show? And what is the EATS thing they keep talking about?'

'Too many questions,' said Christo with finality. 'You stop asking, it no good for you or friend. Just cook, and do as told, okay?'

'Okay, I'm sorry,' Lucas said, worried he might have pushed it too far. The last thing he wanted to do was ruin their chances of going to Rome. 'I like cooking with you Christo. I think you're a very good chef.'

Christo smiled at this, a real smile this time and his face lit up changing him into someone totally different. 'You good cook too,' he said.

Chapter Twelve
Chicken Bombshell

'You have to cook a chicken dish tonight boys,' said Feathers, and the skin on his forehead crinkled up showing he was serious. 'We all agreed at our meeting earlier that as much as we like the vegetarian dishes you create, a real chef must cook with meat.' He stared at Tucker who had slept really late, but managed to drag himself out of bed in time for lunch. They'd all finished and it was time to clear up.

Lucas looked at Lady P and Leonardo on the other side of the breakfast bar nodding in agreement. He wondered about the meeting, whether it was all their idea to get the boys to cook chicken or just Feathers's, if Leonardo had sat in the throne.

'How are you going to feel once you get to that school and all the other children can cook meat and you don't have a clue?' Feathers said, pushing his dirty lunch plate in Lucas's direction. Lucas picked it up and took it over to the sink where Tucker had started to wash up.

'You may have stood out as a good cooks at the orphanage,' Feathers said. Lucas gave Tucker a look. *Why did they keep calling it that?* 'But in Rome you're going to be surrounded by children who can all cook jolly well, you don't want to start at a disadvantage.'

Larks knew that made sense, but how was he going to cook meat? The thought of it made him shudder.

'We could do fish?' Tucker suggested, talking to them over his shoulder. 'There's some pink fish…

'Salmon,' Lucas quickly whispered at him.

'Right,' said Tucker, 'There's some salmon in the fridge. We can cook that?' Tucker really was a top mate, even if he did like to sleep.

Lady P did a little snort of laughter that came out of her nose, she and Feathers turned to Leonardo. Tucker went back to washing up the lunch dishes. There was a pause.

'Salmon tonight, okay,' The Big Man said at last, his chins wobbling. 'But tomorrow you cook chicken, no arguments.' His voice was like a grown-up in charge – firm and final. It meant that Lucas would just have to get used to the idea or kiss the opportunity of chef school goodbye. Lucas looked at Tucker up to his arms in soapy dishwater, grabbed a tea towel and went to help. He didn't want to mess this up. They had to get to Italy.

Chapter Thirteen

Night Exploring

The covers got tangled in between Lucas's legs as he twisted and turned, trying to sleep. He sat up, rubbed his eyes and swung his legs out of bed. He got up, pulled on a jumper and a pair of trainers, crept quietly down the landing and tapped on Tucker's door. Nothing. The whole of Mouthful Mansions was sleeping.

The long dining room was spooky at night, lit up by the moon, the chairs had eerie shadows. Lucas walked through it quickly, into the kitchen and opened the huge fridge. It glared a cool blue light outwards, revealing the pale chicken breasts waiting for him. All Lucas could see were the chickens they had once been, pecking about, scratching at the dirt. It seemed wrong – yet he wanted to be a real chef didn't he? *Have to think about something else.*

He found a thin, black torch in the third drawer down in the utility room. Lucas tried it out; shining it around the white cupboards and sinks, then headed for the library, making the torch beam bounce as he ran.

He shone the torch over the pinned wall map and the shelves of serious-looking books. He tried pushing and pulling at a few, looking for a secret passageway, but soon got bored. Then he remembered the secret side door.

Picking up a bundle of books to use as doorstops, Lucas ran all the way back and wedged the door of the utility room open.

It was dark, very dark, but not that cold. Using his torch he made his way along the side of the mansion, in through the secret door and down the curly stone steps. He thought about dungeons and torture chambers, scaring himself to make it more exciting.

The staircase was wide and the ceiling high. There was a smell of the same disinfectant that they used in the school bathrooms. Lucas hoped it wasn't a load of toilets that he was exploring – that would be rubbish.

He counted twenty-three steps down then it flattened into a corridor that led off straight ahead. He guessed that he was walking right underneath Mouthful Mansions. The corridor widened out into a cave. Dug out of the walls were six cages, big enough to be called prison cells. Lucas scanned the three cages on either side. The bars were wedged into the stone at the front and in between them. The cells on the right-hand side were empty, except for piles of clean straw. The rest were swept clean and the smell of disinfectant was strong.

There was a noise. Footsteps. Someone was coming. He shone the torch into the cages, looking for somewhere to hide. Shadows of the bars crept up the walls and still the noise of the footsteps came. Lucas had to shut off the torch, or be caught.

He plunged himself into darkness. There was a startled cry. The footsteps stopped and instead came a tumbling sound. Whoever was after him was falling down the steps and into the corridor. They must've been using the torchlight to find their way. Lucas switched it back on and shone it up out of the cave into the corridor and right into Tucker's face.

'Easy,' Tucker said, shielding his eyes as he lay at the foot of the stairs.

'What are you doing here?' Lucas asked, nearing him.

'I saw the torch light from my bedroom window, came down to see what you were doing.'

'You scared me half to death,' Lucas said.

'And now you're blinding me.'

'Sorry.' Lucas took the torch beam off his friend's face. 'I knocked and you didn't answer.'

'So you thought you'd just nose about without me?' Tucker started getting to his feet.

'Well, you said you didn't want to get caught snooping about. Anyway, I know you love your kip.'

'I've already said about this morning, I was tired, end of.' Tucker swished his hands through the air as he made his way over to Lucas who was stood in the cave.

'What do you reckon these are for?' Lucas was shining the torch over the cages.

'Must be from before,' Tucker said. 'Perhaps they used to keep animals in here.'

'Used to? Look at them, the straw is clean and sniff the air.'

Tucker started sniffing, 'School loos.'

'Exactly – it's being kept clean.'

'What's down there?' Tucker gestured towards the corridor.

'Not been yet, come on.'

They walked, past the cells, keeping the torch light ahead. The cave fell back into a tunnel-like corridor and after a bit they came to a T-junction.

'Which way?'

Tucker headed to the right.

It wasn't long before the tunnel widened into a horseshoe-shaped cave. Lucas shone the torch about. A round wooden table stood in the middle with four, big, sturdy-looking matching chairs set neatly around it. A dresser was set against the one flat wall stacked on top with a variety of cups and plates. Lucas opened the top drawer of the dresser.

'Look at this,' he said, pulling out a blue folder.

'Hey,' said Tucker getting closer, 'look at the label: EATS 23.'

Lucas opened it up. 'This is the same folder that Christo had under his arm.'

'We might be able to find out what all those EATS meetings are about. Perhaps they plan the shows or something.'

'Not with these they don't,' said Lucas, showing Tucker an old square photograph of an upturned turtle shell. 'This is a recipe for turtle soup.'

'They can't serve that up on *Dinners to Die For*.'

Lucas stopped looking through the folder because he heard a distant rumbling of voices. 'Listen,' he whispered.

'Someone's nearby,' Tucker whispered back.

Silently Larks put the folder back. Keeping the torch beam low they made their way towards the noise. It led them back down the tunnel and straight on, past the left that went back to the cages. The corridor ended in a dark wood-panelled door with metal trimming and studs. It was like a door to a dungeon. A flickering light from behind it came through cracks and knots in the wood. The noise was louder, but still quite faint. Lucas switched off the torch and knelt down, putting his eye up against a big crack. Tucker found another spy hole a little higher up.

It was hard to make out but Lucas could see a white tiled floor. The light was bouncing off it, in time to the mumbling noise. He tugged on Tucker's pyjama leg.

'TV!' he mouthed.

It was the first TV they'd seen since coming to Mouthful Mansions. The last time had been the cartoon in the limo. That seemed a bit odd seeing as they were in the house of TV celebrity chefs.

He tried to tune in to what was on the telly but it sounded boring. He stood up next to Tucker and chose a new spy hole, a crack about shoulder height. It was thinner, but from moving himself around he worked out they were looking at a kitchen. It looked identical to the one upstairs. *Could it be a sort of back up?* he wondered. He couldn't see the TV itself, but guessed by the way the light was bouncing off the worktops that it was up on the wall somewhere.

He felt a tug at his jumper.

'Christo,' Tucker mouthed at him.

It was Christo! Why was Christo in a secret kitchen watching television in the middle of the night? Lucas could feel his heart beginning to thump harder. As if he could hear it, Christo turned and headed towards them. They couldn't be caught; they'd be sent back to Brocken House. Clutching the torch, Lucas turned and ran back down the corridor; Tucker was right behind. They flew past the cages and took the stone steps two at a time. There was no noise behind; Christo couldn't have seen them. Tucker pulled out the books that were wedging the door open.

'Close one!' he said, breathing hard.

'We need to be in bed, sleeping,' Lucas said, walking quickly back to Mouthful Mansions, 'That's the only way we can get out of this.'

'I'll never sleep now.'

Lucas thought it was unlikely that Tucker would ever have trouble sleeping, but he had an idea.

They made it back through into the utility room and Tucker picked up the second book wedge. Lucas went over to the bread cupboard and opened it.

'You will sleep if you eat some of these,' he said, and in his hand he was holding the Darkest Devils.

Chapter Fourteen
TV Crew

Lucas had a groggy wake-up, the kind where you have to pull yourself through the layers of sleep like swimming up from the bottom of a dark lake. There was a puddle of drool on his pillow and his right cheek was squished flat. He touched his hair. It was flat on the left but sticking straight up on the right. It probably matched the flattened cheek, as if he'd been rolled out like pastry. One of his arms was still asleep from where he had lain on it. He was still wearing his jumper, so was sweaty all over, and his mouth was as dry as a cracker.

Once his arm painfully returned to the land of the living, he staggered into the bathroom, ran the cold tap and drank deeply. Thirst quenched, Lucas stuck his face under the water flow. That woke him up!

Shaking his head dry, like a bear, he padded back, sat down on the side of the bed and looked down. There, staring up at him from the rug was the reason for the groggy wake-up: the newspaper package of mushrooms. Tucker and Larks had both eaten four of the Darkest Devils and they'd worked like sleeping tablets. He scratched at his face, wondering how Tucker was feeling and if he was up yet. It was doubtful.

Getting onto his knees he looked closely at the mushroom collection. They were all nicely dried out, which he knew changed their flavour quite a lot. He planned to take out the Darkest Devils then crush the other mushrooms up and keep them in jars as seasoning.

As he was thinking this he moved the mushrooms about with his fingers. An eye of an orangutan peeked out from underneath. Lucas picked up the newspaper and gently tipped the dried mushroom mix into an open envelope. He slipped the envelope into his jacket pocket that hung on the back of the door. Then sat down and read the article properly:

Further Illegal Importation of Exotic and Endangered Animals Into the UK

The police are said to still be investigating the continued illegal importation of exotic and endangered animals and plants into the UK. The detailed and highly specialised operation has created a number of promising leads, although no arrests have yet been made. Although there is no official statement, the police believe that the importation is being carried out by a secret, criminal organisation which they are close to uncovering. Importation of exotics is very lucrative and it is believed that the organisation is supplying plants and animals to UK-based collectors on a demand basis.

This hideous trade has been going on for a number of years, but due to growing public concern over seriously critical numbers of certain species left in the wild, the police have stepped up the investigation into the crime.

It is believed that the latest animal to be imported alive is a female orangutan. She was stolen from a rescue centre in Sumatra where she was recovering from naturally occurring injuries. The World Wildlife Fund (WWF) is said to be seriously concerned for the welfare of the ten-year old orangutan that they named Sheba. The police and the WWF are encouraging anyone with any information to contact the following number: 0845 223 223

A spokesman for the investigation said, "It is not easy to import such a large animal alive without detection from the authorities. It is highly likely that a member of the public may have seen or heard something unusual or has some kind of information that could be very useful to our investigation. We would encourage anyone who thinks they can help us find Sheba, or has any information in regard to continued illegal importation, to contact the helpline number as soon as possible. Thank you."

Sheba looked sad in her picture. Lucas stroked her face gently with his finger wondering where she was. Distant noises outside made him drop the newspaper and rush over to the window.

The front courtyard was filled with white vans parked around the spitting mermaids. The TV crew! They must be here to film the show.

Lucas rushed to get dressed, smoothed down his hedgehog hair, brushed his teeth and grabbed the door handles. His bedroom door was locked! He rattled the handles, trying again, but the door was definitely locked.

'Tucker,' he shouted, running to the far bathroom wall that stood between their rooms. Lucas banged on it hard with his fists. After a while he stopped. A soft banging came back, like a delayed echo. Tucker must be locked in too. He'd be freaking out! If only Lucas could talk to him.

Larks ran over to the window, banged on it and shouted out. Nobody heard, nobody looked up. He tried to open it, but it was still locked. There was a lot of activity down there and people walking about. Leonardo was waddling around laughing and clapping someone on the back. Lucas banged for ages, but everyone just carried on loading up equipment. They were going already? Just how long had they been asleep? He needed them to look up, but they carried on as if the boys didn't exist.

Lucas stopped for a moment to think, touching the top of his badge. He could pick the lock of his door, but watching below he realised he was too late. The white vans drove off over the drawbridge. What was going on? This was not how it was supposed to be. They should been in Italy by now. Why did it feel like things were going wrong?

Chapter Fifteen

Chicken Anyone?

It was Feathers, not Christo, who came to let Lucas out. He could hear the chef mumbling to himself as he unlocked the door.

'Ah, Lucas, you're up and awake,' he said when he saw Lucas sitting on the bed fully dressed. 'Glad to see it, very glad.'

He came ambling into the room all arms, legs and nose and took Lucas gently by the arm, leading him out onto the landing.

'We need to just let the other one out,' he said.

'You mean Tucker?' Lucas asked, a bit huffy.

'Yes, yes,' he said fumbling with the key to Tucker's door. He managed to unlock it and Tucker came flying out like a tornado.

'Why?' Tucker demanded, staring at Feathers and

breathing so hard Lucas thought for a minute he might hit him.

'Yes, yes,' said Feathers who barely even noticed the state Tucker was in. The skinny giant led the way down the corridor to the stairs. 'Sorry about locking you both in like that, dear boys,' he said over his shoulder at them, 'But you were so very asleep. Up last night midnight feasting I think?' He turned and gave Lucas a little wink.

'Calm down,' Lucas mouthed at Tucker who looked pumped enough to even have a go at Flymo.

'Something like that,' Lucas said to Feathers. 'I couldn't sleep because I was worried about cooking meat.'

'Ah, I see.'

They started to walk downstairs.

'I went to talk to Tucker about it,' Lucas lied, glancing at his best mate who looked a bit calmer. 'We were up for hours. I suppose we must've slept late.'

Lucas gave Tucker a sneaky thumbs up, and he did one back. Feathers didn't see.

'You did indeed boys; you slept very late, right through the morning. When we couldn't wake either of you we had to lock you in. We'd started filming, you see, and if you came flying down the stairs in the middle it would cause all kinds of problems.' The chef kind of tumbled down the stairs as he talked. It was as if he weighed nothing at all.

'Filming for the TV can be such a complicated business,' he carried on over his shoulder, 'Everything has to match.' He flung his long arms out as he spoke. It was almost like he was trying to take off. 'The light has to be the same; all the things have to line up just so. If you charged in it could've been disastrous.'

He opened the doors and gestured for them both to go through first.

'You do understand, don't you boys? It wasn't what any of us wanted, locking you up like that, it felt horrible to do. We care about children; it was why we ran the competition. We can see what great little cooks you are, especially you Lucas, and we all want you to succeed.'

Lucas looked at Tucker, who shrugged and nodded at the same time. Larks felt the same. It made sense what Feathers said, and he liked being called a "great little cook". Their places at that school had to be waiting for them.

'And about that other thing,' he said, still ambling along past the banqueting table, 'I know neither of you want to cook meat but it's vital really to being a chef. You can't go through your training and not cook with meat. It wouldn't be fair on you to send you to that school without any experience. We're going to start with something easy. Just a little chicken breast, no blood or gore, just simple white meat, nice and clean. What do you say?'

They had reached the kitchen, Leonardo was pleased to see them, even Lady P was sort of smiling too. They did seem to care about them, Lucas thought.

He looked at Tucker. 'What do you think?'

'Let's go for it,' Tucker said.

'All right, we'll do it, we'll cook the chicken.'

'Bravo boys,' said Lady P and punched the air.

Leonardo started clapping and Feathers hopped

87

about from one elongated foot to the other. 'They're cooking chick-chick-chick-chicken folks; they're cooking the chicken.'

Christo turned his head around and gave Lucas an unexpected look. It was almost like Christo felt sorry for him. The twisted chef turned away quickly, but Lucas couldn't forget it. It made him wonder what Christo was doing in the secret kitchen.

Cooking the chicken was not nearly as bad as Lucas thought it would be. Christo showed them how to slice and prepare the meat and Lucas made a fresh sauce from the dried out mushrooms that they'd found from foraging, leaving out the Darkest Devils of course. Obviously Lucas didn't eat any, but Tucker did. He said it was 'awesome.'

Phil Feathers was wild about it; Lucas had never seen him so happy. He was practically dancing about the place. It was pretty funny. Tucker loved it. Larks wondered if Feathers might choose to do it as one of his recipes on *Dinners to Die For*, he liked it that much.

'Delicious boys, marvellous, glorious chick-chick-chicken. I love it. It's simply divine!'

After dinner Leonardo asked Larks and Tucker in a nice way if they would carry on helping Christo with the cleaning. They told him it was fine because they were used to helping out at Brocken House, so Christo, Tucker and Larks spent the rest of the day polishing and hoovering. Tucker and Lucas never did get a chance to talk on their own, but now that Italy was back on the cards, it didn't seem so important anymore.

Chapter Sixteen
Wednesday

The next day was another round of breakfast and lunch, plus tonnes of cleaning. Later, Tucker was told to clean the upstairs bathrooms and Lucas was sent outside to forage for ingredients to go with the lamb dinner. It was a gorgeous day but Lucas was worrying about how much more meat he would have to cook before they could get on that plane, so didn't notice the weather.

He found a tonne of wild garlic and a rosemary bush that had taken over an old garden bench. After picking what he needed, Lucas wandered around the side of Mouthful Mansions looking for more plants.

He came, by chance, to the secret side door to the cellars and as soon as he recognised it his heart began hammering. Checking over his shoulder he pushed it open and peered inside. There were the stone steps, curling away into the darkness, just like before.

'What, what? What's this?'

Lucas jumped out of his skin and pulled away from the door. Lady P was stood behind him carrying two enormous planks of wood over her shoulder. They must've been heavy, but she carried them as if they were made of foam.

'Um, err,' Lucas stuttered.

'Don't bother going in there, boy,' she said, meeting him squarely in the eye with a hard stare.

'Where does it lead to?' Lucas asked, hiding his face behind the rosemary and garlic.

'Dungeons,' she said then laughed throatily. 'Dungeons are not safe places for little boys to explore. Stick to the plants, eh? What have you got there?' she asked, eyeing the herbs. 'Something for dinner?'

'Yes', Lucas answered, wondering why she lied about the dungeons, 'It's garlic and rosemary to have with the lamb.'

'Lamb? Getting braver every day, aren't you, Lucas Larks?'

Lucas didn't want to think about the lamb or what she might mean about getting braver.

'What are you doing with those?' He freed a hand and pointed to the planks balanced on her broad right shoulder.

'Going to reinforce the hidey.' She gestured with her gun into the wild forest behind her.

'What hidey?'

'Ah, good sign that.' She winked at him. 'If you've not spotted me in there then neither has the vermin.'

'How do you reinforce it?' Lucas wanted to keep her talking. She looked so odd in her tweed outfit, the planks of wood on her square shoulders, the gun in her hand. She didn't seem like Larissa Partnum-Nokes off the telly, the chef who cooked with game; this woman was a short, stout hunter who had just told Lucas an outright lie.

'Interesting question Mr Larks, well I use bale twine, fantastic stuff. I always keep some about my person.'

'What's bale twine?'

Lady P laughed. 'You city boys,' she said, 'you know nothing. It's good strong string; usually yellow.' She rested her gun against one of her stumpy legs, then reached into her pocket and pulled out a handful of the string to show him. 'It's fabulous!' she announced.

'So, your hidey – that's somewhere you wait to shoot rabbits?' Lucas hated the idea, but he wanted to try and understand why she did it.

'That's it boy, right on the money you are. I keep still and quiet in there and when they come out it's bang, bang, rabbit pie for tea. That's one tactic, but you can always flush them out, lots of roaring and shouting and then you shoot the little blighters once they make a break for it.'

'Why do you like it so much?'

'The waiting, the stalking, the thrill of the chase, nothing quite like it, it's a sport like no other. You should give it a go. Might change you into a meat eater. Animals always taste better if they're running away. Besides, the whole place is swarming with vermin. I'm doing the world a service, getting rid of the horrid, furry little breeders. Terrible pests you know, they destroy everything.' She stopped, the chat suddenly over. She picked up her gun and strode off, rustling off into the undergrowth and raising Shaun into the air to say goodbye.

Lucas couldn't even look at the lamb, let alone touch it. He had to secretly tell Tucker what needed to be done, all under the unwavering stares of the three celebrities. It seemed pretty obvious that Lucas was the real chef out of the two of them, but Tucker tried his best. Christo knew, Lucas could tell by the way he looked at them when they whispered together. Luckily he said nothing, just got on with preparing the dessert. None of these people were who they seemed, Lucas thought. He pretended to drop the rosemary on the floor and Tucker stooped down next to him.

'We need to talk,' Lucas whispered.

'What about?'

'Don't you think things feel a bit weird?'

'Maybe.'

'We're cooking really early tonight too, what do you think that's about?'

'It's a Wednesday,' said Tucker.

'*Dinners to Die For*,' they said together.

'What's going on down there?' Lady P demanded, 'We need to see all the cooking you do. Come, come, don't be shy, get on with it. Lucas, you were telling Brian how to rub the rosemary into the cutlets.'

The boys popped back up and Lucas tried to smile at her but it felt wrong, sort of plastic. They carried on, the three of them, in silence and managed to get the job done. The buzz Lucas had had about cooking for the chefs was gone. As he watched them gobbling down the lamb he tried not to think of it as a little, white fluffy creature skipping around its field.

The celebrities finished the dinner and began shuffling off. Even Christo disappeared without staying to eat with them, or help clear up. It felt secretive. It was like the feeling you get when you see a group of kids whispering together and laughing a bit and then looking over at you. Not nice. At least Tucker and Lucas were on their own and could talk properly at last.

'They've gone to watch it for definite,' said Tucker, eating the leftover lamb.

'I reckon you're right.' Lucas helped himself to some of the vegetables. 'Do you think they're keeping us apart on purpose?'

He shook his head. 'They wouldn't have left us on our own now if they were. I didn't sign up to clean toilets though, since when is that a prize?'

'Yuk. Is that what you've been doing?'

Tucker nodded, but carried on eating, 'The bonus is, I got a good snoop around Leonardo's bathroom. He definitely dyes his hair – I saw the packets.'

Lucas laughed.

'And,' he added, 'he's got loads of the same suits.'

'Truth?'

'Yeah, they're all hanging up together in his wardrobe.'

They ate. It was so quiet. It was like that a lot at Mouthful Mansions. Lucas didn't like it much; he was used to noise and lots of kids about. He missed FB too.

'I wish we could watch the show,' Lucas said.

'We should've been on it,' said Tucker. 'You'd think they would want to announce us as the winners, or show us cooking, or something.'

Lucas chewed at a piece of asparagus. 'It freaked me out when my door was locked. You must have been in bits.'

'Totally. I was this close to picking that lock.' Tucker squinted at his pinched fingers, 'I hate feeling trapped.' He shuddered.

The memory of Tucker teaching Lucas how to pick locks flashed into his mind. The two of them, heads together bent over a padlock and a pin. It was a good feeling, like they were a team.

'I thought about picking it too,' Larks said, 'but I didn't because it would be like giving away a secret weapon or something.'

'I know what you mean, like not telling Leonardo about the sleepy mushrooms.'

'Exactly.' Tucker always got what he meant. At Brocken House sometimes you had to have secret weapons. They needed them. 'I knocked at the window for ages, but nobody looked up. It's like no one even knows we're here.'

Tucker grinned.

'What?' Lucas asked, he knew that look.

'Lets just say, I've taken precautions,' Tucker said.

'You're being mysterious, my friend.'

Tucker tapped at the side of his nose. 'I thought Miss Downs ought to know we were staying on here a bit longer, so I sent her a postcard.'

'Genius!' His best mate was the business.

Tucker tilted his head to the side, 'Not just a pretty face.'

They'd finished eating, so Lucas pulled on the rubber gloves ready to wash up. He felt much happier now that Miss Downs knew they were both still at Mouthful Mansions. Lucas trusted her more than anyone else in the world, except Tucker. Then he had an idea.

'I know where we can watch the show.' He pointed in his washing-up gloves at the floor underneath their feet.

'What if Christo is there?' said Tucker.

'It's not just Christo we need to worry about.' Lucas was scrubbing at the baking tray. 'Lady P caught me snooping in there and warned me to stay away.'

He told him quickly about their little chat.

'Maybe we shouldn't go back then.' Tucker looked worried.

'Don't be a chicken,' Lucas said, 'Come on, don't you want to watch the show?'

Tucker nodded and the decision was made.

Chapter Seventeen

Dinners To Die For With A Twist

They ran all the way, only stopping to listen at the door, peeping through the same cracks as before.

'Coast is clear,' said Tucker, stepping back and slowly turning the big handle. Together they pushed the heavy door open.

The kitchen was deserted. Lucas hurried over and opened the first top drawer he saw. It was full of cutlery, exactly the same as the show's kitchen upstairs, but there, on the top, was the TV remote.

'I wonder where they're all watching it,' Lucas said as he fumbled with buttons.

Tucker didn't have time to answer as the TV screen jumped into life showing Lady P frying something pink up in a heavy based pan.

'Wicked,' said Tucker, 'We've only missed the first half.'

Lucas turned the volume down low and checked over his shoulder.

'Such a simple salmon dish of fresh lime, coriander and butter, but I bet it packs a punch,' Lady P was saying.

'They were the ingredients we used,' Lucas said.

'She's cooking your salmon, Larks!'

Lucas's tummy flipped over. Neither spoke as they watched Lady P begin making lemon cheesecake. Lucas couldn't believe it! She did everything exactly as he had. She was cooking his recipe on telly – how good was that?

'That's why she wrote everything down so carefully and asked me all those questions.'

'Look at that!' Tucker pointed at the starter on the screen.

'Mushroom Mayhem!'

'Hat trick Larks, she's done all three!'

The friends high-fived one another, then watched them gobbling up Lucas's recipes. The camera was on Feathers working his fork around his enormous nose. It was brilliant.

Lady P did a quick reminder about how people could get the recipes and all the merchandise the celebrity chefs sold. Next Leonardo's flabby face filled the screen, his chins wobbling as he talked.

'He's going to talk about us now,' said Tucker pointing a finger towards the Big Man.

It seemed funny to see Leonardo on the telly now that the boys knew him in real life.

'I'm a very happy to say that our competition winners have settled beautifully into their new life at the culinary school in Rome.'

Tucker and Larks did a double take, their smiles vanished.

'We are very proud and wish them all the best.' Leonardo smiled, big and broad into the camera.

'But...how can we be there already when we're still here?' asked Tucker.

'A reminder that next week is the last in the series of *Dinners to Die For* live from Mouthful Mansions, but don't worry, we will be back again for brand new series in the New Year! From all here: good night and a happy cooking cook-a-cookers!'

Lucas switched off the television and put back the remote control. 'I'm starting to get a bad feeling.'

Tucker shook his head, 'Don't worry Larks, it's no big deal. Probably just like the other day when they had to lock us in. It will be some TV thing. They have to pretend we're already there.'

'But why?'

Tucker shrugged. 'How should I know?'

They were quiet for a bit and Lucas was thinking about all the unanswered questions that were starting to fizz inside his head. He looked around at the copycat kitchen.

'What is this place?' he asked.

'I've been thinking about it,' said Tucker, 'I reckon they must use it as a back up for filming the show, like if one of the ovens breaks, or whatever.'

Lucas nodded, 'Yeah, I thought that too, but it doesn't explain the cages, or that EATS 23 file and the funny little round room.'

Tucker ran his palm over the worktop. His skin looked darker than normal against the bright white of the secret kitchen. 'Nobody's around now,' he said, 'I suppose we could snoop about, see if we can get some answers.'

Good, thought Lucas and they started opening some of the cupboards. All the ones with plates and pans were exactly the same as upstairs. It felt like a relief, but then they moved onto the food cupboards.

Inside the tall, thin kitchen cupboard next to the fridge, the one that pulled out as soft as a whisper, Lucas found labelled tins.

'Look at this, Tucker.' He turned the tin in his hands so they could read the label together: Powdered Panda Paw.

Tucker looked at Larks, his face all scrunched up as if he'd tasted something disgusting. He reached into the cupboard and took down another tin whilst Lucas opened the one in his hand. It gave off a horrible smell of dried-out meat and earth mixed together. He peered inside. It was half full of a fine brown powder like coffee.

'That stinks,' he said. 'Get a whiff of that.'

Tucker put his nose inside the tin. 'Yuk.'

He put it back and took down another. 'This one's labelled Black Rhino Horn Resin.'

'And this is Sei Whale seasoning,' said Tucker, opening it and taking a sniff. 'Smells like dried fish and the air at the seaside.'

Lucas opened his tin. Inside was a disgusting sticky black gloop. 'I'm not sniffing that one,' he said and closed the lid quick.

They put the tins back and eyed the fridge instead.

The first thing he saw glowing in the blue fridge light was an egg box. Something told Lucas the eggs inside wouldn't be from chickens. He gently lifted the box. It was labelled Leatherback Turtle Eggs.

'Can't be, can it?' said Tucker, leaning over the box.

Lucas opened it and inside were six white eggs almost perfectly round like ping-pong balls.

'They can't be real turtle eggs can they?' Tucker asked again.

Lucas shrugged and starting to feel a bit sick, put them carefully back into the fridge. Tucker looked around the fridge shelves a bit more. There were more tins, like the ones they'd found in the cupboard. Tucker spun a couple of them round to read their labels: Amur Leopard Stock and Grated Mountain Gorilla.

'Don't open them Tucker, I'm feeling sick.' Lucas took a step back from the fridge.

Tucker closed the fridge and opened the freezer. Inside, Lucas could see some labelled plastic containers, the sort you get from a Chinese take-away. Tucker picked up the top one and read it out, 'Vaquita Steaks.'

Lucas had no idea what that was. Tucker put it

down and picked up another, 'Mashed Black Spider Monkey.'

Larks's hands were beginning to shake and he could feel sick rising up to the bottom of his throat. Tucker still had his back to Lucas and he reached further into the freezer pulling out an enormous tin foil wrapped package from the shelf below. He turned it over and read it to himself then looked over at his shoulder to Larks. His eyes were wide and bulgy.

'What is it?' Lucas asked not wanting to hear the reply.

He turned back to the freezer and put the package back. 'You don't want to know, mate.'

'Tell me.'

'Sumatran Elephant Ears,' he said and the closing of the freezer was the full stop.

Lucas staggered backwards hitting the breakfast bar counter behind and gripped the edge to stop the world from spinning. He rushed over to the sink and gagged. Nothing came up, but he felt a bit better. He ran the tap with cold water and washed his face.

'We should get out of here.' Tucker looked as freaked out as Larks felt.

The boys fled back down past the cages and flew up the stairs. The door was shut.

'We forgot to wedge it open,' Lucas said desperately. He felt up and down the door, but there was no handle on the inside. They were trapped.

Tucker gave the door one last angry shove. 'There must be another way out. Christo came in another way.'

Slower this time, the boys made their way back

down past the cages and through the heavy door into the kitchen. There were two other doors.

'You take the right, I'll take the left,' Lucas said running over to the left door at the back, trying not to think about the horrible things hidden around them. He opened the door but it was full of cleaning stuff.

'This way,' said Tucker.

The door opened straight into a wide, illuminated staircase. At the top there was another door with a latch on the inside. Tucker lifted it, pushed it open and they stepped out into a whole new room. It was filled with furniture that looked like it was made of straw. They ran to the door at the other end. It led out behind the staircase into the entrance hallway. Lucas closed the door behind them and they ran up the stairs to his bedroom. He was glad Tucker followed him in; he didn't want to be on his own after what they'd just seen.

Chapter Eighteen
All A Bit Fishy

'EATS is something disgusting isn't it?' Lucas said when the two boys were lying on their backs in their pyjamas, on top of the bed covers. Lucas had had to go with Tucker to his room to get his night things, but he was glad it wasn't just him who was scared.

'I don't want to think about it,' Tucker said. 'I just want to go to sleep.'

'But we've got to find out what's going on.' Lucas pushed himself up onto one elbow and looked at his best friend. Tucker had his eyes shut, but his face was scrunched up.

'We should just keep our mouths shut and get to Italy quick,' Tucker said, and turned onto his side facing towards the wall.

Lucas lay back down. 'I think we should spy on them.'

'No way, Larks.'

'They don't know we've found the kitchen, or that we've seen the show, we can just play along, then when they have one of their secret EATS meetings we'll sneak along and listen.'

Tucker looked over his shoulder. 'We've done too much spying already Larks and it's not done us any good. If we keep on with this they're going to send us back to Brocken House.' He turned back to face the wall.

'You can't go to sleep, Tucker.'

'Watch me.'

Lucas sighed, but let it go. Whenever things got tough Tucker slept and woke up when it was all over. He might be able to turn off his brain, but Lucas couldn't stop thinking about all the things they'd seen in the kitchen. Something horrible was going on and it looked like it was down to Larks to find out what.

Lucas was only sure he'd been to sleep when he heard Christo shouting and banging on the bedroom door. He dragged himself out of bed to let him in.

'Why you here?' said Christo, pointing a long bruised finger at Tucker.

Tucker stretched and yawned but didn't answer.

'Breakfast in five.' Christo stretched out his fingers.

'Wait,' Lucas said. Christo turned back, peering at him from somewhere near his armpit. 'Did you watch *Dinners to Die For* last night?'

'Did you?' Christo spat back.

Lucas glanced at Tucker who had panic written all over his face.

'Five minutes,' Christo said, and left.

Tucker barely let the door shut before he was up out of bed and shouting. 'What did you say that for? Now he knows we know about the kitchen.'

Lucas shrugged. 'I don't think he's in on it.'

'In on what?'

'On EATS, whatever EATS is.'

'Earth to dopey.' Tucker tapped on the side of Lucas's head with his knuckles. 'Christo is the creepiest out of the lot of them AND he was the one who took the EATS 23 folder from the table AND we saw him in the secret kitchen with all those horrible ingredients – of course he's in on it.'

Lucas clapped his hands, 'I knew it.'

'Knew what?' Tucker had backed off and was starting to get dressed. Lucas did the same.

'I knew that you thought things were fishy round here.'

'Dur, it's hardly normal to have elephant ears in your freezer, but I just don't want to go messing about and spoiling our chances.'

'So, let's just do another postcard to Miss Downs,' Larks reasoned.

'Why?'

'Tell her we're still here. After the show everyone is going to think we're in Italy. Don't you think that's a bit weird?'

'Very weird.'

'So?'

'Oh all right.' Tucker handed his friend the postcards and stamps. 'But you can write it and sneak it into the box, I did the last one.'

Lucas took the postcard and quickly wrote: *Miss Downs. We're still at Mouthful Mansions. Things are weird here. Can you check that we are still going to Italy? Also is eating elephants and turtle eggs against the law? Please tell FB I miss him. L&T.* He added the address of Brocken House and stuck on a stamp.

'Might as well leave these in here,' Lucas said, putting the postcards and stamps into his bedside drawer.

'Come on,' said Tucker pulling open the door, 'And hide that thing quick.'

'What about our teeth and hair?' Lucas asked putting the postcard to Miss Downs into his inside pocket.

'After breakfast.'

Chapter Nineteen
A Night Delivery

The boys got through another day of cooking and cleaning. Lucas managed to sneak out and get the postcard in the box. There was no mention of Italy, but Tucker was acting like the teacher's pet, jumping to every command and still refusing to spy on the chefs.

That night, Tucker went back to his room and probably fell straight to sleep but Lucas couldn't stop feeling that everything was turning bad. The competition was like a delicious-looking peach that when you picked it up to eat it you found it had secretly rotted away underneath.

He was starting to wonder if the competition was even real. Perhaps they had brought them to Mouthful Mansions to give them new recipe ideas for the show.

Maybe they just wanted them for free cleaning. Lucas didn't want to be forced to cook meat and made to clean toilets for the rest of his life. It might break him, like it had Christo. He kept on thinking about EATS too; what was it and why were all those ingredients in a secret kitchen underneath them?

A distant noise out the front of Mouthful Mansions made Lucas get out of bed and across to the window to investigate. A big lorry was parked out the front and Lucas could see three, no, four men around it. They were trying to unload something from the back. It was just after two in the morning – this was definitely no grocery delivery. Lucas couldn't see properly because of the way the lorry was parked; he needed a side view of the castle. Tucker's room had the perfect spying window. Slowly Lucas opened the door of his bedroom, put his head out and peeked up and down the hallway. It was clear so he crept out silently and quickly hurried up to the next-door bedroom. Lucas didn't bother knocking, just went straight on in. Tucker was awake and up at the window.

'Shh,' he said, even though Lucas had barely made a noise. Lucas smiled to himself as he joined his friend, and the pair of them watched out of the window as four men, all dressed in black, wearing big army style boots, heaved at a big wood-slated crate with: THIS WAY UP! plastered all over it in red ink. The boys couldn't hear them, but it was obvious from all the kerfuffle that the crate was very heavy. Eventually, using long poles that the men threaded through the highest slat holes, they lifted the crate up and carried it on their shoulders. The slats were spaced wide enough to get a tantalising look at what might be inside. The boys watched the men walk slowly up the side of the mansion, struggling with the crate. Lucas knew they were headed for the side door with the curling stone steps that led to the cages. Then he saw the hand and felt instantly sick.

There was no other way to describe it, it was a hand, bigger than Lucas's head, black and wrinkled like old leather. It came slowly out of one of the gaps between the slats and gripped at the wood. There was no mistaking the tufts of orange fur and the human-like way the animal was trying to steady the crate from rocking. Lucas knew what was in that crate and it made everything a whole lot worse.

'Is that a monkey in there?' Tucker whispered.

'It's Sheba,' Lucas said.

'Who?'

'Sheba, the stolen orangutan. Come on,' Lucas pulled at Tucker's arm, 'I've got something I forgot to show you.'

They crept back into Lucas's room. Larks found the newspaper and handed it to Tucker, whose lips moved as he read it.

'I'm sorry Larks,' he said, 'I was wrong, we should've started spying on them yesterday, just like you said. We'll start now.'

Lucas felt a surge of feeling for his best friend and wanted to do something to show it, but he couldn't hug him, Tucker would hate that.

'We have to try to act normal,' Tucker said, 'They can't know what we've found.'

Lucas nodded. 'Yeah. And we need to tell Miss Downs about the orangutan.' Lucas reached into the drawer and pulled out the postcards. 'They're going to eat her, aren't they? That's what EATS is, some kind of horrible club that eats rare animals.'

Tucker nodded, 'I think it must be.'

'I bet she's going in one of those cages and that's what the kitchen is for.' He shuddered. 'I thought they were cool, like cooking heroes, but this…? It's disgusting…it makes them monsters.'

Tucker nodded, 'Monster chefs.'

'We have to tell someone, tell the police.'

'We can't, we've only got the postcards.'

Lucas looked down at the postcard. It was pathetic; there had to be another way.

'What about Leonardo's phone?' Lucas said suddenly. 'He has it in his top pocket. I saw it on the first day when he put the postcard you gave him inside his jacket.'

'Seriously? How are we supposed to get hold of that?'

Lucas shrugged and started writing: *Miss Downs. You have to call the police as soon as you get this. We've just seen Sheba, the stolen orangutan from the news being delivered here. We think they are going to eat her. Please come and get us. We're scared and don't know what to do. Lucas and Brian.*

Chapter Twenty
Full English

It was scary creeping out in the dark to post the card to Miss Downs, but when the boys came down to breakfast the next day Lucas felt better knowing they were trying to do something about what was hidden under their feet.

'Good morning Leonardo,' said Tucker and smiled at the grotesque animal eater as if he was his best friend. 'Morning Larissa, morning Phil. And good morning to you Christo!'

Lucas wondered if he might be overdoing the acting a bit.

'Morning, budding chefs,' said Leonardo as the boys went around the other side of the breakfast bar. 'What you cook us today? Some bacon? I love the full English, don't you Larissa?'

'Rather, especially on a Sunday morning with the newspaper and a good strong mug of tea.'

As the monsters rumbled on about nothing Tucker and Larks washed their hands and put on fresh aprons.

'Can you cook the meat?' Lucas whispered to Tucker from their usual secret spot down by the fridge door, 'I don't think I can.'

'I do meat.'

The boys turned to see Christo looking down at them. 'I watch and I know,' he said, his voice secretive.

'Know what?' whispered Tucker.

'You no cook,' he said looking at Tucker, then his eyes flicked to Lucas, 'But he good cook. Don't worry, I no tell Leonardo.'

Christo leaned over them into the fridge and pulled out a huge mound of sausages and bacon.

'You do egg,' he said to Lucas, 'and you do toast,' he said to Tucker.

Tucker made the "phew" sign, like he was wiping sweat off his forehead, Lucas did it back to him, then they got on with what they had to.

Watching Leonardo shove countless sausages into his mouth was revolting. Lucas wondered how many animals had died to make him so fat. Now Lucas knew the truth, Leonardo seemed disgusting.

'Try some?' Leonardo asked Lucas, snapping him out of his thoughts.

Lucas shook his head.

'You only eat plants?'

He nodded, unable to trust his voice.

'So quiet these days, Lucas,' said Feathers. 'You're not changing your mind about becoming a chef are you? We're still arranging things in Italy for you and Brian. You do still want to go don't you?'

Lucas opened his mouth but couldn't say anything. All the questions he had would give them away.

'We're very excited about Rome,' said Tucker. 'We're just a bit worried about speaking Italian. We wondered if Christo might be able to teach us some before we go?'

Lucas wondered where Tucker was going with this, as they'd not talked about it. Leonardo lapsed into a string of Italian directed at Christo to which the wizened man shrugged and said a few words back.

'It's no problem,' said Leonardo. He smiled. 'He can teach you some now when you clean up.'

The three chefs got up and began wandering off. Lucas elbowed Tucker and nodded to their backs. Tucker raised his eyebrows and went to join Christo at the sink. Tucker didn't understand; they had to follow the chefs! This was their chance to find out about EATS and the orang-utan but Tucker was busy learning the words for plate and cup and fork in Italian. Lucas was hopping from one foot to another, not sure what to do.

'You go get those mushrooms,' said Tucker over his shoulder and he winked at his friend, 'I can finish up here.'

Larks pulled off his apron and hurried after the chefs. He just caught the back of Lady P's jacket as she disappeared into the room filled with straw furniture.

113

Lucas knew they were headed to the little room for their EATS meeting. He ducked out of the front door, came to the side door and looked around for a wedge. Using a big stone, he stopped the door open and hurried quietly down the stone steps.

The orangutan was in the middle cage on the right as Lucas walked in. Until his eyes got used to the light, she was just a shadow. She was in the furthest corner with her back to him, her face turned to the wall. Lucas had never seen a wild animal like her before. It was sad to see her caged up, but at the same time amazing to be so close. Lucas stood and stared for while. He was more star struck by her than when he'd first met all three of the celebrity chefs. He forgot that he was supposed to be spying. A real, live orangutan, close enough for him to touch; Lucas felt that magic.

She turned her head so that she was side-on and Lucas saw the outline of her face. She had to be the same one from the newspaper. He softly said her name.

'Sheba.'

She knew it straight away. She cocked her head then turned herself around so that she was facing the boy. The straw rustled when she moved.

'So, it is you then Sheba? I'm Lucas,' he tapped his chest and said 'Lucas,' again.

She watched him closely. It was just like she was listening and trying to understand. Feeling brave, Lucas swung open the door to the cage next to Sheba's and climbed inside. The ground of the cage was solid, dry earth. The smell of the school loos had gone and the new animal smell was nice; kind of homely.

There was some loose straw inside which was clean and dry, Lucas bunched it together to make a sort of cushion that he sat on and leaned his back against the cool earth behind. It was very peaceful and Lucas felt calm. He closed his eyes and listened to all the tiny sounds the orangutan made, only inches away.

It was as if Sheba was an old friend and they were getting to know one another again. It was comfortable and felt safe – almost as if Lucas had come home. He kept his eyes closed for a bit longer.

Chapter Twenty-One

Spies

Lucas had no idea how long he slept but he woke to the sound of the monster chefs' voices coming from a distance. He could tell they were on their way from the secret kitchen, towards him. As quietly as he could, Lucas pulled up the rest of the straw, making a heap around him. Sheba was interested in what Lucas was doing. He put a finger to his lips to try and warn her, and then buried himself deep underneath the straw. Curling up into a ball he lay really still. Lucas could hear the chefs talking about him and Tucker.

'Who cares what they think they know,' Lady P was saying, 'It's not like they can tell anyone anything is it?'

'But they might've found the monkey.' That was Feathers.

'They won't have found the monkey,' said Lady P. 'It only arrived last night, besides I probably scared that Lucas boy witless with my dungeon talk. They'll not have come down here since the monkey arrived.'

'I still think we should do it sooner than we planned,' Feathers answered. Lucas imagined him ambling along the corridor, stooping to avoid scraping the top of his pointed head. 'The good-for-nothing brats could've worked it all out by now, and that means we're not safe anymore.'

Brats? So they didn't like children after all, Lucas thought, *and what was all that stuff about not being safe? Maybe that's what Lady P meant. She was talking about keeping EATS, whatever EATS was, a secret.* That's why they always shut the boys out whenever there was a delivery and why they were locked in their rooms when the TV crew were there.

'You no panic about the boys, Phil,' said Leonardo. 'Panic does no good. You running this way and that way like a chicken with no head.'

Lucas heard Lady P's throaty laugh.

'How long we do EATS now?' Leonardo was asking.

'Eight years, maybe more,' said Feathers, 'But animals are different, they can't talk can they? They can't tell anyone about EATS, but the boys…'

'And in those eight years', interrupted Leonardo's Italian drawl, 'do we have any sniff from the police?'

'Well, no, but like I say…'

'Eight years, the police no care, they too busy catching the real bad guys. Nobody cares about the odd animal here and there. All the people, they too busy driving cars and making the money. We care more about animals, we care how they taste.'

It was Feathers's turn to laugh. It was a sort of humphy puff that probably came out of his nose. 'And EATS was an inspired name,' he said.

'You only say that because you thought of it, Phil,' said Lady P.

'Endangered Animal Tasting Society? It's inspired, you said so yourself.'

'Pish, pash.'

Endangered Animal Tasting Society: EATS. This was the secret criminal gang that the police were looking for. They were the ones bringing the endangered animals into the UK. They weren't even collectors – they were eating the animals. Sheba was going to be eaten! Lucas was shaking with anger but willed himself to stay still; one tiny little move and they would spot him.

'It is good name. And we no worry because the boys will be dealt with, all in good time. They no tell anyone about EATS, they no have chance. Don't forget our plans for them.' Leonardo's voice was loud they had to be right outside the cages. Lucas barely dared to breathe. He imagined them all staring at poor Sheba and hoped she wouldn't give him away.

'But if we did it sooner…' began Feathers again, but he was cut off sharply by Leonardo.

'Enough about boys. Look at this instead.'

'My God, that monkey's a whopper,' said Lady P. 'Good job we've got the freezer, it'll take a month to eat.'

'It really is big. How are we going to cook the thing?' asked Feathers.

'Perhaps we could ask Lucas,' said Lady P then lapsed into her horrible scratchy laugh. 'So ridiculous of you, Leonardo, to choose the one vegetarian entry to win the competition. Cooking with mushrooms. Good God, how utterly pointless. The other one, he can't cook at all.'

'Stupid woman,' snapped Leonardo and his voice was deep and cruel, 'I no choose for their cooking. They orphans, no one cares where they are. Everyone think they in Rome. No family to come a look, look looking.'

Lucas knew he shouldn't care what any of those monsters thought about his cooking, not one of them was a real chef, but Leonardo's words hurt and he hated him even more.

'Even though I can't stand snivelling children,' added Feathers, 'I have to say I rather like all that stuff Lucas makes, especially when you add some chicken.'

'Oh do shut up about chicken Phil, it really is quite fatiguing,' snapped Lady P.

'Only if you shut up about vermin.'

'Both of you shut up!' barked Leonardo. 'Follow me, we sit down and decide how to chop up and cook the big orange monkey.'

'If we follow you, we'll be here all day,' mumbled Feathers to himself.

Lucas listened to the criminals muttering to each other as they made their way back down the tunnel. It sounded like they were heading for the round room. He thought about EATS going for eight years and wondered how many rare creatures those monsters had munched their way through. They were cold, heartless murderers. Lucas had to get out and talk to Tucker; they had to stop them. They couldn't let them eat Sheba.

As quietly as he could Lucas emerged from the straw. Sheba calmly sat watching, her brown eyes taking in every movement Lucas made. He raised a finger to his lips again in warning then crawled silently to the cage door, pushed it open and swung himself down to the floor below. He shuddered to think how close he was to being caught in there, but at least they now knew the truth.

Lucas found Tucker polishing the bannisters.

'You've been ages,' he said, 'I thought they'd caught you.'

Lucas shook his head. 'I fell asleep in the cage next to Sheba and I heard everything.' Lucas picked up a duster and pretended to be cleaning with him. 'EATS means Endangered Animal Tasting Society.'

'Whatie?'

'They ship in endangered animals and eat them.'

'That's what all those tins and packets were of then.'

'Yeah, and the folder with recipes and that map with pins in. They're all down in that little room now talking about how to cook Sheba.'

'We've got to stop them, when are they going to do it?'

'I don't know, in the next few days. That postcard to Miss Downs might be too late, we need to get to a phone.'

The boys polished, their hands working as quickly as their brains. Then Tucker found the answer.

'Why don't we just run away?' he said simply. 'It doesn't matter the gate is locked, we can climb it, and if we can't climb it, we can pick the lock.'

'That's it, my friend, you're a genius. We'll just run away.'

They carried on polishing, working their way up the stairs, thinking about a plan. Christo stopped them with a single word: 'Pranzo.'

Tucker started packing up the cleaning things. Lucas looked at him and without having to ask Tucker said, 'Lunch.'

Chapter Twenty-Two
Trapped

A whole day somehow passed. The chefs had no idea that the boys were onto them. Christo was treating Tucker like his new son and chirped away to him in Italian. Luckily, Christo cooked all the meat too.

Lucas couldn't look at those criminals without feeling sick. Knowing that Sheba was caged up was horrible, but they had to wait for their chance to climb that gate.

'You cooking very well boys,' said Leonardo, even though it was obvious that Christo was doing most of the work. 'No long to wait before Rome.'

Christo clanged the pans. His face had gone white. Leonardo said something in fast Italian to him. Christo said nothing; instead he took off his apron and threw it on the floor. He looked at Lucas, then Tucker and strode out of the room.

'What on earth did you say to the man?' asked Feathers.

'I remind him what what.'

'Oh, I see.' Feathers turned to look at the boys. 'I think our Christo is getting a little attached to you two, and you'll not be with us for much longer will you?'

Lucas looked at Tucker but could tell he was just as confused. If they went to Rome they could tell anyone they liked about EATS; the driver on the way to the airport; a policeman; even the pilot if they wanted to. Lucas wondered why they were still pretending. Perhaps they were still thinking of sending them because they really thought the boys knew nothing. Or even if they did they couldn't say anything as they wouldn't be able to speak Italian, but then why was Christo teaching Tucker? None of it made any sense.

Tucker had said it was best to go to their own rooms that night, so nobody suspected the great escape.

At two in the morning, Lucas's door silently opened. He had packed his bags and was dressed, ready. He followed Tucker down the stairs, happy to have him in charge. Using the utility door to be quieter, the boys ran out onto the grass. They only got halfway down the drive. There was no point going any further: the drawbridge was up. Lucas thought about the steep, slippery sides of the stinking moat and knew they were trapped.

Tucker began to panic. 'What about a raft?

Couldn't we build a bridge across or something?' He was frantically pacing about on the grass.

'Shh.' Lucas glanced up at the dark windows behind. 'We don't want to wake them up.' He was thinking about Lady P's gun.

'You said something about planks of wood from the hidey – what about them?'

'The moat is too wide, way too wide! The banks are too steep for a raft.'

'But, but...but, we can't be trapped Larks, we can't!'

'Shh,' he said again, 'let me think.'

Tucker paced and Lucas tried to think of a way out, but it was no good, the boys were stuck.

Chapter Twenty-Three
Worst Morning Ever

The next morning was horrible, the worst by far. Neither of them had slept. Tucker was pacing all night, saying how he had to get out. Lucas kept thinking about the postcards and how it was up to Miss Downs to save Sheba.

Lucas managed to get Tucker to calm down and the boys agreed that they'd try to keep pretending. Their only hope was to keep quiet and wait for Miss Downs to get help.

In the morning the horrible villains were waiting to be fed, like sheep at the gate. Lucas was about to put on his apron when he saw the postcards displayed on the breakfast bar. Instantly he felt sick.

'What are you meaning by this?' Leonardo said, his voice low and stern.

Lucas stared at the postcards and felt his eyes fill with tears. That was their plan to escape. Their plan had failed. Nobody knew they were still at Mouthful Mansions. Everybody, except these four crazy people, thought they were happily living in Rome. Without those postcards getting out into the real world, the boys were as much prisoners as Sheba, the orang-utan.

To make matters worse, the chefs had read the postcards – they knew what the boys knew.

'We take you in, we give you good home, let you cook whatever you want, you live in luxury, you have no school, no horrible time and yet you do this,' Leonardo jabbed a finger at the postcards 'Hateful boys. Now we have to take off nice hats, put on nasty hats. All trust gone.' He thumped his fist onto the breakfast bar surface.

'This is how it to be. You cook what we want when we want it,' Leonardo ticked off one of his fingers on his left hand with his right, 'you clean what we want you to clean when we want it cleaning,' he ticked off a second finger, 'you ask no more questions,' a third finger went, 'you keep mouth tight shut,' a fourth and final finger was ticked off.

Lucas raised his gaze to look up into Leonardo's face. His friendly smile had changed into something horrible and frightening.

'You have no choices. You try to get away, we lock you up. You refuse to do things, we no give you food or water. You do what we say then everybody happy, but you try to cheat us then we get angry and hold you like a prisoner.'

Lucas looked at Lady P. 'Don't blow this chance, boys. Leonardo is being highly reasonable. There are dungeons you know, I wasn't joking about that.'

Lucas looked at Feathers. 'You really shouldn't have written those postcards. What happens here is nobody's business. Mouthful Mansions is our home and we'll do what we like in our own home. You, as visitors here, should have shown better manners and given us more respect.'

The chefs were revolting – how could Lucas ever have thought of them any other way? He had been blind. He thought these people were his heroes, but they were cruel. Leonardo wanted to gobble up the world and let everyone else do the hard work to make it happen.

Christo and Larks cooked breakfast in silence. Tucker was in shock and stood in the corner of the kitchen, his face set in a vacant gaze. Lucas's hands shook as he sliced and chopped. Leonardo ate four or five times the amount of the other two. The sight of him throwing bacon into his massive mouth made Lucas feel sick.

'Delivery coming in next hour,' Leonardo said, a drip of brown sauce running down over his chins. 'You not be here. You must see nobody. You try anything then we know about it and we punish you. We always watching.'

The three monsters shuffled off. Lucas looked at Christo up to his elbows in dirty dishwater and saw his own life ahead, stretching out as an endless road of slavery.

'Come on,' he said to Tucker, once the evil trio were out of earshot.

'Where go?' asked Christo.

'I'm going to introduce him to my friend, Sheba.'

'Sheba who?'

'The orangutan.'

'No, you no go there. It no safe…he…' Christo fell into Italian but Lucas was pulling a stunned, silent Tucker out of the door of the utility room and ignored him.

Chapter Twenty-Four
A New Friend

'Come on, Tucker.' Lucas tugged at his friend urgently. Tucker was barely moving and mumbled something Lucas couldn't understand. If Tucker saw Sheba, he might stay strong, for her sake.

After pulling and pushing for ages, they finally got to the side door. Tucker stood there swaying about, like a baby tree in the wind. Lucas propped open the door with the big stone and pulled him towards the steps.

'You have to keep it together, my friend,' he told him. 'Get down the steps without falling and you'll see why.'

Tucker tumbled his way down the stairs, they rounded the corner and there she was.

'Isn't she amazing?'

At the sound of Lucas's voice Sheba shuffled over to the front of the bars. Her eyes were mesmerising – deep and sad. She reached a hand to the bars and Lucas copied her movement. Their fingers touched. Her skin was thick, like old leather. They looked at one another properly, taking in every detail of each other's faces.

'We have to save her, Tucker,' Lucas pleaded. 'Remember what the article said? She's one of the few left in the wild. We can't let them eat her.'

Tucker was staring straight at Sheba but it was as if he couldn't hear his friend, or even see the orangutan properly. He looked far away, somewhere Lucas couldn't reach him.

'I know we couldn't climb out and I know that our postcards didn't get through, but they keep talking as if they are still sending us to Rome.'

Tucker said nothing; he just looked dazed. Lucas carried on, but his words ran off his friend, as if he was waterproof.

'When I was hiding in here', Larks pointed to the cage, 'they said about it not being long. So maybe they're thinking once we're in Rome we won't be able to say anything to anyone. Maybe we're not trapped after all, but Sheba, she is trapped and we need to get her out.'

Lucas didn't really believe these things, but even if Tucker had heard him, he didn't show it. He just stood there gaping at Sheba. Lucas would have to rescue them both.

Chapter Twenty-Five
Carrots and Broken Noses

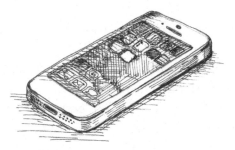

Tucker was worse than useless for the rest of the day. He stumbled about all over the place moaning and groaning.

'What's happening to the fool?' asked Lady P.

Christo babbled in Italian to Leonardo who waved a huge hand through the air. 'Put idiot to bed, he no cook anyway, he no good,' he said.

Christo and Larks helped Tucker up the stairs to bed. He fell down gratefully against his pillows, pulled the cover around him and was asleep within minutes.

'He might need a doctor,' Lucas said to Christo as they stood over Tucker watching him.

'Leonardo no let stranger here.' Christo beckoned for Lucas to follow him out.

Everything was falling apart; Lucas needed to call for help. The only phone he'd seen was Leonardo's mobile. He kept it on him all day in his inside pocket, but what about at night? He had to charge it. Lucas thought about the phone charging on Leonardo's beside table. That was the answer! He had to play dumb until tonight when he could sneak out, steal the mobile and make that call. It would work – it had to.

Having such a good plan made things easier. Lucas kept his mouth shut, like he'd been told to, and his eyes down. He cooked their meat, but didn't watch them eat it. All the time he thought about that mobile sitting in Leonardo's pocket and how the whole nightmare would be over once he got hold of it.

Suddenly the phone buzzed from Leonardo's dinner jacket. It made Lucas jump, like he'd activated it with the power of his mind. Lucas watched Leonardo pat his pocket, pull out his phone and peer at the screen with piggy eyes.

'Ah', he said, 'it's the orphanage.'

Lucas's heart jumped into life. Leonardo clicked his fat fingers and like lightning Feathers whipped round the other side of the breakfast bar, grabbed Lucas from behind and clamped one of his huge bony hands over the boy's mouth. Lucas didn't struggle at first, after all he was playing dumb, but this was it; Feathers was weak. Larks wouldn't have to wait to steal the phone; this was his chance to free Sheba and to save Tucker. Lucas watched Leonardo nod his head then press a button to answer the call.

'Yes, this is Leonardo De'Largio,' he said, then paused to listen to the other person.

Lucas wondered who it could be on the other end. Probably Mrs Corneal, or maybe Miss Downs? The thought of the staff at Brocken House made him feel strong. His heart was hammering so wildly that he hoped Feathers couldn't feel it.

'It's not a problem, you not disturb me, I gave my mobile number to you... yes, I have heard from them, they very happy at the school.... yes they both cooking well...that's fine, you can send the records to me, I will forward them on.'

Lucas didn't need to hear anymore, this was his moment. He bit down hard on Feathers's hand, who screamed and let go.

'We're still here,' Lucas shouted as loud as he could. 'They're holding us as prisoners, me and Tucker and Sheba the orangutan...' He couldn't get any more words out as Lady P leaned over the breakfast bar and punched Lucas square on the nose.

She took the boy completely by surprise and he screamed out in pain. He could hear the crunch of the bones in his nose the moment her jewelled knuckles hit his face. His whole head throbbed and he could feel blood gushing out of his nostrils. Lucas screamed and keeled backwards, arms floundering around. It was Feathers who grabbed him again, trying to pin his arms down to his sides. Lucas was spluttering and could see the blood dripping onto the white tiled floor at his feet.

'Hold him,' commanded Leonardo. He was

clutching his mobile in his hand, a hand so big that the phone looked like a toy. Lucas hoped that whoever was on the other end had heard him. Help had to be on its way.

It probably took all of Feathers's strength, but he held Lucas tight. He'd stopped screaming now, but his eyes swam with tears and the pain was horrible. There was a strong stinging in his nose and a deep throbbing inside his head, right down the cheekbones and into his teeth.

'You're cowards,' Lucas said (though it sounded more like "dowerds" seeing as he couldn't breathe though his nose). 'She will have heard me and the police will be coming.'

'Poppycock! You want me to tie him up with some bale twine Leonardo?' Lady P reached into her pocket and pulled out her little bundle of yellow string.

Lucas looked at Leonardo, he was laughing and shaking his head. Lady P put the string back in her pocket. Leonardo's laugh was so big it made all his flab ripple. 'I cut off call just as Phil screamed out like a drop, she no hear you.'

'Drip, that's the word you're thinking of, Leonardo, not drop,' corrected Lady P.

'Hey,' said Feathers, 'I'm not a drip. The nasty brat bit me really hard, look at my hand.' He shoved his hand in front of Lady P, and Lucas was proud to see a big red welt forming on the base of his fingers. 'I think that will scar. I hate children, nasty little parasites. We should just do the job, Leonardo.'

'You just big baby, getting beaten up by little boy,'

said Leonardo and Lady P laughed. It sounded like nails on a cheese grater.

'Now I have to call the nice lady back.' Leonardo looked down at his phone that began vibrating in his hand. 'Oh wait, no I don't, she calling me.' He looked at Lucas with pure hatred. 'Keep him quiet.'

Lady P took a T-towel, pulled it through Larks's mouth and tied it at the back of his head. The boy was struggling to breathe now and there was no way he could shout out. He was forced to listen to their chance of escape slip away once more.

'Hello again...yes, I know...sorry about that, Phil Feathers he very clumsy and he burn his hand...no, he okay now, he's patching himself up but I have to stop call to help him...yes thank you for understanding, now where were we?... Yes... Lucas... he very good cook... Oh yes, Brian, he learning too...they teach many sorts of cooking, they will learn for many years... yes that's right, they learning Italian, will stay in Italy I think... yes good happy ending, I agree... okay, no problem...bye then...ciao.'

He turned off the phone and slipped it back into his pocket. He nodded at Feathers who let go of Lucas and then another nod at Lady P who undid the gag.

Larks spluttered a bit then his fingertips went up to his poor, sore nose.

'Oh, it's broken,' said Leonardo, 'I can see from here. Lady P have a big punch no?' He smiled at the horrible woman who walked back round to his side of the breakfast bar carrying the blood-covered tea towel in her hand.

'You stupid boy,' Leonardo said, 'now we have to take away freedom.'

'You already have,' Lucas said and he tried to look strong and not afraid.

'You and friend had lots of freedom but now we keep you locked up at night and all the time you not cooking and cleaning. You finish cooking now, then eat, clean up and we lock you inside your room.' He nodded to Feathers who patted Lucas down. He took the penknife from his trouser pocket and put it on the worktop. He found the forgotten envelope of left over mushrooms, but after checking it gave it back.

'Clean up there,' said Leonardo gesturing to the sink and pocketing the penknife.

Lucas walked over to the sink, next to where Christo had gone back to calmly stuffing chicken breasts with soft cheese. He barely looked at the boy, but there was something there, something different from before. Was it pity? Lucas wondered about him and whether he was someone they could trust. He didn't help Lucas, but then he didn't help the monster chefs either.

Lucas cleaned up as best he could – at least the bleeding had stopped. He said nothing, just went back to chopping the carrots. He was going back to acting dumb but his mind was racing.

Leonardo reached over a tree-trunk arm, took a carrot and chewed on it. He was smiling his horrible smile and Lucas could see the mashed-up carrot between his teeth.

Chapter Twenty-Six

Mobile

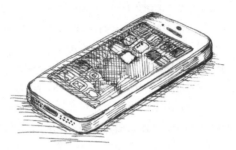

Before Larks was locked in his room, he took a tray of food to Tucker. Feathers came to unlock and re-lock Tucker's door.

'See, boy,' he said, 'you've cost your friend's freedom as well as your own.'

Lucas ignored him. Tucker was still fast asleep. Lucas wished he could sleep away the horrors too. He lay the tray on his friend's bedside table and tiptoed out of the room.

Lucas had set the alarm on his watch for one o'clock in the morning, but there was no way he could sleep. He lay under the covers on his back, fully dressed staring up at the curtained canopy above with his nose and head still throbbing painfully. Everything he had seen was churning around in his mind, like dirty washing.

Mouthful Mansions was silent for a long time, but when his alarm finally buzzed he suddenly didn't want to do it anymore. He was scared. Every time Lucas had tried to do the right thing it ended badly – and now he had a broken nose and a locked bedroom door from his efforts.

Lucas wondered what horrible punishment they might do if they caught him again. He thought about Tucker in his enchanted sleep and pushed the covers away; he had to do this, not for just for him, but for Tucker and for Sheba. She did not deserve to die just because they wanted to eat her. The world was not just theirs; they didn't get to decide everything. She was a real creature, an endangered animal, what they were planning on doing was evil. Lucas had to stop them and he was on his own.

The monsters may have taken away the penknife that he used for foraging, but they had no idea about his badge. Lucas took it off the lapel of his jacket and carefully bent the pin so that it was ready.

He remembered Tucker's lesson: 'picking locks takes skill, my friend, but most of all you need patience.' Larks pushed the pin into the lock and felt around. He had to get exactly the right place and push precisely the right amount. He fiddled around for a few minutes, carefully listening for any sign of life outside. Eventually came the satisfying click of the lock and Lucas eased out his badge, bent back the pin and secured it on his jacket. The door opened easily.

Trying to ignore the throbbing in his head and the

desire to turn back, Lucas followed the landing, keeping closely into the shadows by the wall. He padded along silently in his socks. He came to Leonardo's closed bedroom door, took two steadying deep breaths, and with a shaking hand turned the handle.

The door opened softly and he peeped round to see the giant monster laid sprawled out on his back on top of his covers, still fully dressed in his dinner suit. His mouth hung open and he was snoring out rumbles of thunder.

Lucas scanned the top of the bedside table; yes – there was his mobile, charging beside his bed. All Lucas had to do was to creep over there and snatch it, call 999 and be out of there. He took a single, silent step inside his room.

'Gnnrrugh,' came Leonardo's horrible gruff snore.

Larks took another step.

'Snnurrrgh.'

He took a third and a fourth step using the snores to cover up any noise he might be making and never took his eyes off the sleeping pig.

Once he was right up beside his bed, Lucas reached out a shaking hand for the phone. Up close, Leonardo was even more revolting. Larks wondered how he could've admired someone so disgusting. The fat hung off him like uncooked dough and his eyes were sunken so deep inside his flab they were almost lost.

Lucas struggled a little to detach the charging wire from the base of the phone. Unfortunately, the moment the cord came away the phone gave a little bleep. Larks froze. The snoring stopped. Without looking back, Lucas tried to run with the phone gripped tightly in his hand but he wasn't moving anywhere.

Leonardo's paw of a hand had Lucas's left wrist tightly grabbed. In pure terror Larks screamed out, even though he knew it would only make things worse.

Leonardo made no effort to move, he just gripped the boy tight and watched him scream and wriggle like a worm on a hook. Larks used the phone to bash at the monster's hand. If only he could get him to let go. He would only need a minute, or less to make that call, but it was like he was made of concrete and couldn't feel a thing.

Leonardo held on to the boy effortlessly. Larks screamed and screamed for him to let go and kept bashing at his hand. His own wrist was hurting badly, and no matter how much he struggled the monster's hold never loosened, not even the tiniest fraction. Lucas was trapped in his vice-like grip, and all the time he remained on his back, staring at the boy with his piggy eyes and smiling that horrible cruel smile.

Lucas's screams roused the other sleeping horrors. In came Lady P, wearing a disturbingly bright pink floral nightie and matching nightcap. Without her make-up on she looked like a grumpy hippo. If Lucas hadn't been so terrified he might've laughed.

'What's all this hullabaloo?' she demanded.

'Mr Larks now escape artist. Take phone off him quick.'

Lady P came over and then Lucas realised his stupid mistake. All that time he could've dialled 999 with the free hand that held the phone, but instead in his panic he'd used the phone to bash at Leonardo's hand.

Lucas swiped the phone with his thumb and instantly the passcode screen flashed up. He just managed to touch the emergency call button before Lady P grabbed the phone and disconnected the call. *Perhaps the call had got through*, he thought, even though he knew it was impossible.

Feathers came into the room, 'What is all the shouting and screaming?' he squeaked.

He was wearing pale blue, striped pyjamas, the ones that button up at the front with collars. His enormous feet were bare and Lucas could see his hairy toes as he ambled his way into the drama.

'Lucas Larks thinks he can just do what he likes when he likes – that's what,' answered Lady P.

'How did the brat get out? I thought you locked him in?' Feathers asked her.

Lucas kept his mouth firmly shut. He was not about to reveal his lock-picking secret to the evil trio.

'I did, I'm sure I did.' Lady P looked puzzled.

'The door wasn't locked,' Lucas lied quickly. 'Go check for yourselves, it was never locked.'

Feathers glanced at Leonardo who nodded and he hurried out of the room almost tripping over his own long legs.

'Take him downstairs and chain his leg,' commanded Leonardo. 'He can sleep next to the monkey.'

He let go of Lucas and pushed the boy so hard that he fell to the floor, landing at the feet of Lady P like a defeated slave. He fell so close to her fluffy pink slippers that the fur tickled his cheek, but he didn't feel like laughing.

Chapter Twenty-Seven

Chained

The noise and sensation of a gentle scratching wove into Lucas's dream and eventually woke him. Sheba was carefully parting his hair, grooming him. It was soothing.

'Oh Sheba,' Lucas said quietly so as not to startle her, 'I wanted to save you and to stop them, but I've fluffed it haven't I?'

Sheba made no sound at all but the grooming carried on. Lucas turned his body slowly so that he could look at her. Her eyes weren't just a solid colour like he'd first thought – they were lots of different browns, in layers, and they were flecked with amber. She pulled back her big lips, showing four yellow front teeth on each row and four scary looking wolf teeth beside them. Lucas hoped she was smiling and smiled back.

'They think putting me down here is a punishment, but there's nowhere else I'd rather be in this dump. I just wish my friend would wake up.'

Sheba put her arm back through the bars and Lucas touched her hand with his first finger. His skin was so white next to her completely black hand.

Her hand was strong; Lucas knew she could just snap his fingers like twigs if she wanted. He traced his finger over the back of her toughened skin. It felt like living leather. He scratched gently in through her orange hair on her arm, which was quite rough and very thick. He could see how each hair grew out and entwined with its neighbour to make her fur. It was so different to FB's soft ginger stripes.

People shared this world with so many other creatures, it didn't seem fair to Lucas that humans got to be the boss all the time.

Sheba had a sort of musky smell but it wasn't strong and Lucas kind of liked it. She pushed her other arm through for more stroking. Lucas sat up and gave her his full attention.

After a bit of arm scratching she pulled them back through, turned and pressed her back against the bars. Lucas scratched her on her shoulders and back. She loved that, he could tell by her gentle grunting noises, a bit like a snuffling pig. The muscles across her back bulged beneath her hair, solid to the touch. It was amazing that such a big, strong animal could be so tender and gentle. How could they want to kill and eat her? It made him fizz with anger. They were the ones that needed to be locked up. Lucas needed to be smarter than before: he needed a proper plan.

About an hour later, Christo arrived with some breakfast and started pushing bananas and sweetcorn through Sheba's front bars. When it came to Lucas's turn he had to unlock the cage door to put the bowl of porridge inside. Lucas was surprised he wasn't being summoned to cook up more meat for the monster's breakfasts.

'How's Tucker?'

'He still sleep. He sleep long time.'

'Did he eat the dinner I left for him?'

Christo shrugged. Lucas left the porridge sitting there, growing a skin. Sheba was eating fast, almost guzzling. Lucas liked watching her face as she concentrated on stripping the outer green shell off the corn on the cob. It looked funny, almost human.

'You eat,' said Christo.

'I'm not hungry.'

Christo made a noise with his tongue, a sort of tut. 'The boss, he want you to eat.'

'Well, just throw it away; tell him I did eat it. What's the difference? What does he care anyway? Worried about me keeping enough strength to scrub his toilet is he?'

Christo made the tut noise again. He rummaged in his chef white pockets, pulled out a piece of paper and posted it through the bars. Lucas unfolded it and started to read, but could only stomach the first two words: Roasted Orangutan. He started ripping up the paper.

'What you do? Stop, he be very angry,' Christo was waving his arms. He fumbled with the key to try and get into the cage to stop him, but it was too late, the recipe from hell was shredded into tiny pieces.

'No, no, this bad, this very bad,' said Christo scrabbling around in the straw, picking up fragments of paper.

'What more can he do to me Christo? I'm not frightened of him, I'm not scared of any of them,' Lucas lied, 'and there's no way he can make me cook Sheba.'

'You have to,' said Christo, pulling back out of the cell and locking the door again. 'What Leonardo want Leonardo get.'

That made Lucas angry, 'No, he doesn't. He's greedy and horrible and...and a murderer! He can't just do what he wants. All this EATS thing, it's illegal you know. The police, they're looking for Sheba, she's in the newspaper. Don't you get it Christo? They're all criminals, I have to stop them.'

'No, no, you can't do.'

'I have to and you can help me, Christo; they trust you.'

'I no help you, you speak too much,' he clamped his bony hands over his ears, like a moody toddler.

Lucas crawled closer to the bars and made his voice all soft and mushy like he used to when he wanted something from Miss Downs. 'Leonardo is just using you,' he said. 'He steals all your ideas. You're a really good cook Christo. The bread you make,' Lucas smacked his lips, 'it's to die for. You're not his slave; you don't have to cook and clean for him and you don't have to do anything for EATS. He can't make you.'

'But he my friend, he help me.'

'That was years ago. You've paid your debt off twenty times over, you don't owe him your whole life. Tucker and me, we'll be your friends. We'll be much better friends than Leonardo.'

Christo stood there looking helpless.

'We saw you one night, down here in the secret kitchen,' Lucas said quietly, watching to see what he might do. 'You hate it here don't you? You're trying to think of ways to get out.'

Christo said nothing.

'If you help us Christo, we'll help you to get out of here too. We don't have to be afraid of them.'

Lucas waited, but Christo said nothing, just stared at the floor. Lucas tried something softer, 'Look at her, Christo.'

They both watched Sheba as she gobbled down her breakfast.

'She's done nothing wrong, she's innocent. She's one of the last of her kind in the wild, she should be there now but she's in here, waiting to be cooked up by those horrible monsters.' Christo flinched at the word monsters. 'That's what they are Christo, they're evil.' He looked unsure. 'Please Christo,' Lucas tried, 'you have to help me. You have to help Tucker.'

147

'No, no, I no listen to you, you make me confused.' Christo backed away and fled along the passageway, leaving Lucas with his cold porridge and a munching orangutan.

Lucas sighed, 'Looks like we're on our own, Sheba.'

Later Feathers arrived, unlocked Lucas's cage door and grabbed hold of the chain around the boy's leg.

'Get up, you horrible, good-for-nothing, blood-sucking leech,' he spat. 'It's time to work.'

Lucas thought about refusing, but his nose was still sore from Lady P's punch and he worried they might hurt Tucker whilst he slept.

Like a chained slave he was led by Feathers up into the studio kitchen where the others were waiting. Christo was wiping the surfaces; Lucas knew he couldn't look at him.

'Chain him up there,' said Leonardo, and Feathers started to lock the end of the chain to a foot of the sink.

'I need the toilet,' Lucas said.

Leonardo rolled his eyes, and then snapped his fingers. Feathers led Lucas to the downstairs bathroom, snapped his chain to the bottom of the loo then left, shutting the door behind him, all without saying a word.

As Lucas washed his face he looked at himself in the mirror. He had smudges of dirt everywhere, his nose was swollen and crooked, his hair had bits of straw in it and was stuck up all over the place, like a toilet brush. He looked a mess. He had to get out, or this was how his whole life would be; forever in chains.

Chapter Twenty-Eight

Sheba

The rest of Sunday was only just bearable. Everywhere Lucas went, the chain, and one of the evil trio went too. They never once took their eyes off him and they wouldn't answer any questions about Tucker or Sheba, or what was going to happen to them all.

After Lucas had cooked and cleaned until he could hardly stand up, he was led back to his cell and given some food and water. He was happy to see Sheba again, but he knew that she didn't have long. Lucas thought about picking the lock of his chain, or at least letting Sheba go, but how would she live? And how could Lucas leave Tucker behind?

Monday was the same, but by the evening Tucker was up! Lucas saw him stagger blindly into the kitchen.

'Tucker,' Lucas said, running towards him as far as the chain would allow. He looked at his best friend as if Lucas were a stranger. 'It's me, it's Larks.'

Tucker said nothing, just stumbled about the place bumping into things like a newborn foal.

'Come on mate!' Lucas said, 'Get it together, yeah?'

It was Christo who guided him to one of the stools; the chefs just laughed at him.

'Stupid fool,' said Feathers. 'Look at the way he bounces off the furniture.'

'He looks like a drunk,' snorted Lady P through her nose.

'You did this,' Lucas shouted at them. 'You did this to him. You told us we'd won, that we were going to Italy, but you just want us here as servants.'

'Oh, we've got bigger plans for you than that, boy,' said Feathers with a sneer.

'Don't give the game away just yet,' said Lady P. 'It spoils the chase.'

Tucker managed to eat a little of what was put in front of him then Leonardo ordered him to sleep downstairs in the cage with Lucas.

'Keep all animals together,' he said.

Tuesday morning dawned and Lucas could hear Leonardo, Feathers and Lady P as they got nearer to the cages. He sat up suddenly. Tucker hauled himself awake and shuffled back so that he was leaning against the wall. He rubbed at his hair.

'You all right?' Lucas asked him.

He still looked glassy, but he gave a little smile and a nod. Relief that his friend was coming back washed over Lucas. A glance over to Sheba told Lucas she was frightened. He tried a smile to reassure her, then she did this thing, this amazing thing, she put her finger to her lips. Lucas copied her and turned to Tucker. He slowly lifted his finger to his lips too. They sat there, the three of them frozen for just a moment and Lucas felt like he might cry.

The cruel trio came into view, Christo was with them. Larks pulled himself next to Tucker at the back of the cage, trying to let the cool earth against his spine steady him. Sheba rustled the straw. Lucas could see she was trying to hide underneath like he had.

Leonardo was carrying an axe, he tried passing it to Christo and a long stream of Italian came flooding out of his cavernous mouth. Christo was shaking his head and refusing to take the axe. Leonardo got angrier, he shook the axe at him and more Italian came out faster and louder. Christo said something back quite softly and flicked his long bony hand in Lucas's direction. The argument went back and forth between them for ages. Leonardo was really angry but Christo just shook his head and wouldn't take the axe.

'What's the matter?' asked Feathers, 'Why's Christo refusing to kill the monkey?'

Leonardo glared at Lucas. 'It's the boy, he's been talking nonsense sense to him.'

151

'We just say nonsense Leonardo, it's not…'

'Don't be correctioning me all the time,' snapped Leonardo, turning sharply towards Lady P, waving the axe in the air. 'I know English, I live here a long time.'

'Well, of course,' said Lady P in a nice enough way, but Lucas saw her tighten her hands into fists. 'I apologise if I've offended you Leonardo. Please do go on, you were telling us about Christo and the boy?'

Feathers was glancing about nervously. Lucas guessed this was not how it usually went. *Good*, he thought, he was glad it was difficult.

'Stupid Mr Larks has big mouth. He tell Christo that he the real chef, that we just steal ideas. Christo now say he no kill the big orange monkey.'

Lucas wanted to scream out, 'She's not a monkey, she's an ape, an orangutan! And you, you're all murderers,' but he kept his mouth tightly shut.

'Oh, for God's sake, I'll kill the damn monkey, you bunch of wimps,' said Lady P and she grabbed the axe from Leonardo's hand.

'Wait,' Lucas said, dramatically and Lady P stopped suddenly, the axe hanging in mid air.

She looked over at the boy, raising an eyebrow. 'You have something to suggest Mr Larks? Or perhaps you're no longer a vegetarian and want to kill the big beast yourself? I hope you're ready for the mess. There's always a great deal of blood.'

'Well…I was going to say something,' Lucas faltered, trying not to think of the mess Sheba would make if she was hacked up with an axe by Lady P.

'Don't listen to him,' warned Feathers. 'He'll twist

your thoughts Larissa; stick to the plan. You go ahead and kill the monkey if Christo won't.'

'I'm not saying not to kill the ape', Lucas said carefully, 'I'm just thinking about making it more…' he searched for the right word. He thought about her with Shaun the shotgun and those planks over her shoulder, 'More…sporting,' he said, feeling pleased with himself.

'Sporting?' she questioned, keeping her gaze on Lucas as she began to lower the axe.

'Just kill the monkey,' demanded Leonardo.

Lady P tightened her grip on the axe, there was a twitch of a nerve in her jaw. 'Go on,' she said to Lucas, ignoring Leonardo's command completely.

'Well, why not let the orangutan go?' Lucas suggested carefully. 'You could hunt it; stalk it out from your hidey. I remember you telling me that animals always taste better when they're running away.'

Leonardo started laughing, Lady P turned sharply towards him, the axe still tightly gripped in her hand. 'What, may I ask, is so amusing?' she spat at him.

'You never kill it.' He wiped a tear from his eye, 'He trick you.'

'I'm a crack shot, of course I'll shoot the thing and it's a damn sight cleaner than hacking the orange brute up down here. The boy has hit the nail on the head, we'll let the monkey loose and I'll hunt it down and have it shot within the hour.'

Lady P marched towards Christo and put out her hand for the key.

'Are you mad, woman?' said Feathers. 'You can't let

a fully grown beast like that loose, look at the muscles on the thing; it will eat us for breakfast.'

'Gobbledegook. You've seen for yourself man that the monkey eats sweetcorn. It's perfectly harmless,' reasoned Lady P. 'But if you'll feel safer I'll fetch my gun and you can all wait upstairs. Watch from the conservatory windows if you like. The whole thing will be done and dusted in no time. Bang, bang, and it's roasted orang-utan for tea.' She mimicked shooting a pretend gun over her shoulder right at Sheba, who still cowered under the straw.

'You no hunt monkey, you kill it here, same outcome. That's it, said Leonardo, crossing his hands on top of one another like a stern teacher.

'Oh no you don't, Mr De'Largio,' said Lady P, pulling herself up as tall as she could. 'I'm getting pretty tired of you making all the decisions. I'm releasing that monkey to make it sporting and I'm doing it now. I never get the chance to hunt big game. Stay if you want, or hide upstairs the choice is yours, but I'm doing it.' She held out her hand again for the key.

Christo looked to Leonardo.

'Don't look at him, he doesn't make the rules you know, we all do,' said Lady P, her voice a bit higher than before.

Christo glanced at Lady P then back at Leonardo.

'You no give her key Christo, you my friend, no hers. It should be you who kill the monkey, you should do what I say.'

Lucas was pleased how this was turning out; an

argument between the monsters was better than he'd hoped.

'Oh, now that really does take the biscuit, Leonardo!' said Lady P. 'Just how long do you expect Christo to fall for that bullying story, eh?'

'Come on Larissa,' said Feathers looking at everyone anxiously and hopping from one foot to another, 'you're touching a nerve now, just keep out of all of that.'

'Why?' snapped Lady P. 'Christo's not stupid. He must've worked out by now that Leonardo put those boys up to it.' She turned to face Christo.

'Keep mouth shut,' demanded Leonardo but Lady P ignored him.

'You know don't you, Christo? You know that Leonardo's not really your friend? He paid those boys to bully you. That was his plan and how he got you to feed him. They only bullied you because he paid them. He told us all about it and he laughed, we all laughed. But you're stuck with us now, aren't you? You've as much blood on your hands as the rest of us. If we get caught, you get caught. No visa, no right to be here at all have you? Straight to prison like the rest of us.'

Lucas couldn't believe it: Leonardo really was a monster. He watched the pain and shock flash across Christo's face. He thought about the crumpled photo in Christo's pocket and all those years of cooking and cleaning, so much so it had twisted his whole body.

'Don't torment him, Larissa,' said Feathers.

'I'm simply asking for the key.' She was still holding out her hand for it.

For those few moments Lucas felt more sorry for Christo than he did for himself, or Tucker, or even Sheba. He had wasted his whole life on Leonardo, the most evil fraud that ever lived. He willed him to give Lady P the key, then like the rising of a perfect cake in the oven, he did. Christo reached into his pocket, handed Lady P the key, then sadly walked away.

'Good decision my man,' said Lady P over her shoulder to him and turned to Sheba's cage. Feathers practically ran out of there, the coward. Only Leonardo was left.

'You make big mistake,' he said to her, wagging a fat finger through the air.

'Poppycock.' She blew a raspberry at Leonardo's back as he waddled away after Feathers.

'You'd better open the side door,' Lucas said and Lady P jumped, as if she'd forgotten all about the boys.

'Good idea Mr Larks, best not have the monkey rampaging through the whole of Mouthful Mansions had we?'

She hurried off and Lucas made his way up to Sheba's bars and held onto them. The orangutan turned towards the boy, the straw falling from her orange fur. She shuffled closer.

'I know you can't understand me, but when she lets you out, go up high into the trees and stay there. You have to hide.'

Sheba touched the fingers on Lucas's hand very gently and looked into his eyes.

'I think she can,' said Tucker, his voice cracked and unfamiliar.

156

'Can what?' Lucas asked, without turning round.

'Understand you.'

There were a few perfect moments before Lady P's footsteps could be heard.

'Door's open,' she bellowed and appeared, flushed and excited like a little kid at Christmas.

She fumbled with Sheba's lock, then opened the door. Lady P stepped back and, using her big bulk, she half-blocked the corridor towards the secret kitchen. She was clutching her gun in her right hand and she was grinning from ear to ear. The axe had gone.

Sheba was unsure at first. She looked at Lucas, then at her open cage door, then at Lucas again. She pulled her lips back, then forward into a perfect O, and then used her knuckles like feet and made her way out carefully through the cage door. Sheba looked briefly at Lady P, who waved her arms and shouted at her, then the amazing orangutan hurried off up the corridor and away.

'I'm counting to fifty, that should give you a sporting chance, then I'm coming after you, you great orange brute,' screamed Lady P, and began counting.

Lucas closed his eyes, willing his new friend to safety.

Chapter Twenty-Nine
The Truth

During the next two scary hours, Lucas listened for gunshots as slowly Tucker began to come back. Lucas watched his friend's body begin to awaken; Tucker stopped drooping, his eyes brightened. It was such a relief to see him become more like his old self.

'I've got a plan,' Lucas told him, once he was positive he'd understand.

'What plan?' Tucker looked worried.

Lucas reached into his jacket and pulled out the mushrooms. 'Do you remember these?' He showed him the Darkest Devils.

'Remember them? They knocked me out.'

'Exactly! We just have to get them into the chefs' food, then once they're asleep we can grab Leonardo's phone and…'

'Call 999. That's brilliant Larks!'

Lucas grinned at him and carefully put the mushrooms back.

'Do you think Sheba will be all right?' asked Tucker.

Larks shrugged, 'I hope so. Lady P hasn't shot a thing since we've been here, but she loves the chase.'

'That was pretty smart of you, Larks, to think of getting her to let Sheba go.'

'Thanks.'

'I'm sorry,' he said, 'that I lost it before. It's just being trapped, I can't…it makes me remember…and I…'

Lucas put his hand on his friend's arm. 'It's okay; don't worry about it, you don't have to tell me anything, or explain. You're back now and we're in this together, yeah?'

'Yeah.'

Lucas had that feeling again, like he wanted to say or do something, but instead he told Tucker the other part of the idea.

'Hey listen, I was thinking, can you pretend that you're still not with it?'

Tucker frowned.

'They won't be watching you so much and they might not even tie you up if they think you're still half asleep,' Larks explained.

Tucker nodded. 'Okay. Whatever you say. You're the man with the plan.'

They heard footsteps; someone was coming. Feathers ambled into sight.

'You've caused a right mess, you horrid brat,' he said to Larks as he unlocked the cage. 'But then I suppose that was your intention?'

Lucas said nothing.

Feathers glanced up at Tucker. 'He's still mute then?'

He still said nothing.

'Silent treatment, is it? Well Leonardo no longer trusts Christo to be left alone with either of you, not that Christo is doing anything that Leonardo asks at the moment. I wouldn't be surprised if that traitor ends up in one of the cages next to you two before long.'

Feathers grabbed Lucas's chain and led him along the corridor. He barely glanced at Tucker who played his part beautifully and ambled behind like an old, friendly dog. It felt good to be able to stand up straight again and Lucas stretched his arms up above his head.

'No time for any of that. Seeing as there's no Christo, you two will need to cook dinner for us, then set up for the show tomorrow. Mind you, I don't know why we're even bothering to bring that one,' Feathers jabbed a thumb over his shoulder towards Tucker, 'Worse than useless if you ask me, but Leonardo said bring him, so bring him I shall.'

Excellent. They were still letting Lucas near the food. He resisted the urge to grin at Tucker. If Sheba managed to stay safe for just a little longer he could save them all. He felt the crunch of the envelope full of dried mushrooms still tucked safely inside his jacket pocket. The plan would work.

Feathers was right, there was no sign of Christo or Lady P, and Lucas had to cook for the other two by himself whilst Tucker swayed about in the corner. It was troubling – they couldn't leave Lady P awake; she was the one with the gun. If she didn't eat the mushrooms the plan might not work.

Leonardo's piggy eyes followed Lucas around the kitchen. The chain was noisy as it dragged along the floor behind. He needed to get the mushrooms in the sauce, or into the meat, but could he risk it with them watching?

'I should listen to you better, Feathers,' Leonardo said, and Lucas hated the way he spoke.

'What did I say?' asked Feathers. Lucas hated him too, especially the way he sucked up to Leonardo.

'You said we should do the job before. If I listen to you, we no be in this mess; one boy swaying about in corner, Christo in big huffy puffy and Larissa running around with lost monkey.'

Leonardo sighed and thumped his huge fist on the breakfast bar.

'And we have live show tomorrow,' he added, shaking his head, making his chins wobble.

Lucas smiled a little to himself. He would do it now, just rub the mushrooms into the meat. He wondered how many he had and if it would be enough. Hopefully Lady P would come in to eat too, and then he'd get all three of them. Once they were asleep, things would be easy.

Lucas began reaching for the envelope. Even if they did notice would it matter? He started going over his excuses: mushrooms, he'd say, just like before. Lucas's heart was hammering as he pulled out the envelope and tipped the mushrooms into his hand. He stopped himself from checking over his shoulder to see if they were watching. Stay casual, don't make it obvious.

'Well,' said Feathers thoughtfully, 'we could always do the job tonight Leonardo. Why keep putting it off? You never know, it might reunite EATS. It could even bring Christo back on side?' He paused, perhaps waiting for Leonardo to say something.

With his heart still thumping Lucas rubbed the mushrooms into the pork. The meat was rubbery and cool. He tried not to gag, or think about dead animals as he dropped the rest of the mushrooms into the marinade. He walked coolly over to the sink, washed his hands. He'd done it! The mushrooms were in!

'I know Christo never really liked the plan for the boys,' Feathers said, 'but doing the job would stop Lucas's meddling once and for all wouldn't it? No boy equals no tittle tattle in Christo's ear.'

Lucas wanted to give Tucker a sign, but when he saw his friend's face it looked worried and confused. Larks stirred the marinade, his hands shaking. To take his mind off the thought of being caught he started to go back over what Feathers had just said, wondering what it meant.

'What are you talking about?' Lucas asked them,

as bravely he could, leaving the marinade and turning round to face them. 'What's doing the job?'

Both Leonardo and Feathers were staring directly at Lucas, a horrible snide look on their faces. Lucas began to feel the blood draining from his body just as Leonardo started to smile.

'Maybe you right, Phil,' Leonardo said. His horrible face was framed with hanging flab.

Fragments of memories started flashing through Lucas's mind as a new, even more horrific idea, began to form. He remembered…

Lady P shaking his hand, '*Glad to see you have some meat on your bones, boy.*'

Leonardo warning Christo not to get too friendly, then a second warning about Tucker…

Christo clunking the pans, the look of pity on his face.

All three chefs checking that neither boy had any family. Calling Brocken House the orphanage. The way they all stared at them hard and made Tucker feel so bad.

Feathers saying how much he hated children.

Lady P telling Feathers not to give the game away when he said they had bigger plans for them.

All their talk about EATS.

Tucker and Larks weren't there to be their servants; they were there to be *eaten*.

Those monsters saw the boys as animals just like Sheba. EATS had *them* on the menu!

Lucas's legs turned to jelly and he collapsed to the floor. Leonardo and Feathers started laughing. Tucker ran over and sat down next to his friend.

'Larks,' he said. 'Larks, come on mate, talk to me.'

Lucas's head was spinning. There were so many clues; they should've worked it out before; they could've tried harder to get away.

'The competition,' Larks whispered to Tucker, 'it was so they could cook us. They want to eat us.'

Tucker didn't understand; Lucas had to make him understand.

'That was why they made up the school in Italy. It was so they could pretend that was where we'd gone, when all the time they had eaten us.'

'You're scaring me, mate.' Tucker looked like he might be sick, but he had to know the danger they were in.

'Don't you get it? We're just like all those endangered animals. EATS just see us as meat to be gobbled up.'

Tucker was finally completely freaked out. They had to get out; they had to leave now.

'Oh dear, dear, Leonardo,' Feathers said, 'I do believe the penny has finally dropped.'

'Stupid boys,' said Leonardo, 'You think we like children? You think we want to help you and save you from orphanage? You think we let you win special competition to send you off to be good cooks?'

Leonardo was enjoying it; he loved revealing what EATS had planned all along. He was proud of it.

'We no pick you because of stupid mushrooms; we pick you because nobody cares about you. We can chop, chop you up, fry you, boil you, grill you and gobble you down and nobody knows. I always want to

164

try to eat human flesh and a child so young and juicy. One day I say to Larissa, I say "ever eat a person", she say…'

'What do I say?'

It was Lady P's voice – she was back. Then Lucas remembered his badge…maybe with Tucker's lock-picking skills they still had a chance to get away.

'I was telling the story about how EATS make such a good plan to eat a child. I was saying to Lucas Larks and Brian Tucker here…'

'Where?'

'Oh, they're here, right here,' said Feathers and laughed again. 'It appears the news of us planning on eating them has come as rather a shock and Lucas has fallen onto the floor. His friend is still in the land of La La. Quite upsetting, especially seeing as Lucas hasn't finished cooking our pork chops.' He laughed again.

Larks hated him. He hated them all. He looked down at the ring around his ankle. There was no way they were going out without a fight. Slowly, without making a sound, he began moving it towards him. The boys were behind the breakfast bar; unless the evil monsters leaned over they couldn't see them. They still had a chance to escape. Tucker cottoned on and leaned over to unpin the badge. They had to stay silent, one tiniest noise and they would kill them. Lucas prayed they would keep talking and give the boys enough time before they made their move.

Then there was the unmistakeable stomp of Lady P as she marched over to them. 'Oh, so the child vermin know their fate. Well I just hope it won't spoil their flavour. On another note entirely, I cannot find that ridiculous monkey.' Lucas breathed a sigh of relief, Sheba was still safe.

'I've been out there for hours. The damn thing has gone up into those trees and I can't see the brute anywhere. You'd think an enormous, ugly, orange thing like that would be easy to shoot, but that thing can climb, I can tell you. It's up there somewhere laughing at me.'

Lucas smiled, good old Sheba. Tucker began to fiddle with lock on the leg chain.

'Seemed crazy to me to let the thing go, just to go out and shoot it again. Why didn't you just shoot it in the cage? That's what I can't understand,' said Feathers.

'That's because you're not a hunter, Phil. You don't understand about giving animals a sporting chance. Where's the sport in shooting the thing when it's right next to you in a cage? I had to let it go, so I could hunt it.'

'And yet…it got away,' added Feathers.

'Well, forget monkey,' Leonardo chipped in, 'and forget this pork rubbish that the boy think he can cook cooka up. He's a rubbish chef, he run quick quick lickety split out of ideas. The time has come.'

Tucker was shaking too much, so Lucas took the pin from him. His hands were sweaty, which made it tricky, but he kept steady, kept breathing in and out and tried not to listen to the evil voices above.

'Oh, how exciting,' said Lady P, and there was the

noise of her rings clashing together as she must've clapped her hands. 'Are we doing it tonight?'

'Yes!' said Leonardo, 'It's a time for EATS to eat boys! I can't stand to see either of their stupid, snotty faces any more days. And they starting to stink worse than the monkey. Lets cook cooka them up tonight. One eats plants, one eats meat, both of them make tasty treat!'

'Oh very good, Leonardo,' said Feathers, encouraging the horrible fat man to go off again.

'Boil them, bake them, roast them, fry them, I no care, we just get them and we eat them.'

'Yes!' screamed Lady P and Feathers together.

The boys heard them start to move around to their side of the kitchen. Just in the nick of time, Lucas felt the satisfying click of the lock. He pulled out the pin of his trusty badge, shoved it quickly in his pocket and the lock on his leg pinged open. Freedom!

Reaching into the nearest cupboard, Lucas pulled out the first thing he could find – a large frying pan. He jumped up from behind the counter and without hesitating whacked Leonardo square across the head with it. Leonardo barely flinched; his flab wobbled from the blow.

'Ho,' he said, 'this boy have some fight.'

Tucker had grabbed a carving fork; he waved it wildly about in front of him. 'Stay back or I'll...or I'll...prod you,' he warned.

Lady P was stalking towards them. 'Aha, so it would seem you're not a mute after all?'

Feathers was a couple of paces behind, hiding behind her like the yellow-bellied coward he was. Both of them had their arms outstretched, and Lady P was smiling broadly.

Larks waved the frying pan from side to side – Kung-Fu style. He wasn't worried about Feathers, but Lady P would take a few whacks to bring down. Then, disaster!

'Use this,' Leonardo said, and he waddled towards Lady P holding her gun. Even she couldn't miss from there.

'Run, Larks!' shouted Tucker, 'run for your life.'

Tucker charged, stabbing the air with his fork. They dodged out of his way and he ran for the door. Lucas jumped cat-like onto the sink and scrambled over the counter behind. He landed on the floor and righted himself.

Turning, Lucas saw Lady P had her gun levelled at him. He lifted the pan in front of his head just as she fired her first shot. It hit the frying pan shield making a loud "ting" noise, and threw him staggering backwards. He steadied himself, dodged Leonardo's hands that were waving about trying to grab him, and ran across the open studio to the door which Tucker had left open behind him.

Lady P fired another shot, which hit the wall. Lucas fled through the door. He could hear the three of them coming after him. Tucker was long gone; hopefully already out and into the woods. Feathers was probably moving the fastest, but Larks knew he was quicker than that ambling coward.

He streaked down through the big dining room,

past the fake gold throne, past the banqueting table and through the open double doors. Another shot was fired just as he hurled himself through. It ricocheted off the wooden doorframe above him.

'Damn those boys,' Lady P said, 'I've got to reload Shaun now.'

'Don't shout it out loud, that's just stupid! Now they know they've got time to get away,' Feathers screeched.

'Don't call me stupid,' she shouted back at him.

Lucas ran through the open front doors of Mouthful Mansions and was away around the side and into the trees beyond. He dropped the frying pan and, lighter now, almost flew, running faster and faster after Tucker. His breath heaved in and out, hurting his chest. His arms pumped through the air and his trainers pounded the earth as he ran for his life.

Chapter Thirty

Running

It was harder running through undergrowth. Lucas scrambled on, not caring if brambles ripped his clothes or nettles stung. He just had to get away and leave the horrors far behind.

When it got too thick to run, Lucas caught a glimpse of his friend ahead, and then watched him trip and fall. When Lucas reached him, Tucker was splayed flat on his face. Lucas flopped down next to him in the dirt. They were breathing hard, pain thundered in Lucas's chest. He strained to listen for any sound of the murderers chasing, but there was only their own heavy breathing. Exhausted, they both lay still, letting their bodies recover.

'They were going to eat us,' squeaked Tucker. 'They were actually going to eat us.'

'That's what the whole thing was about.' Lucas could hardly talk, he gulped at the air. 'The competition wasn't even real. They just wanted to get some kids that they could eat that nobody was going to come looking for.'

'I can't believe anyone could eat another person. It's disgusting.'

'They're seriously dangerous now.'

'They always were,' said Tucker, 'we just didn't know it.'

As soon as they caught their breath, the boys got up and moved on, running when they could. They struggled on past the trees, through the brambles and weeds. There was a stink of rotting fish that got stronger until the boys were suddenly at the moat, skidding to a halt, knocking loose dirt down its bank. Lucas peered over. The edge was deadly steep; a sheer, slippery drop that was three or four times his own height. It seemed worse here than it had from the drawbridge. Lucas looked about; there was no sign of the child murderers, but he was overwhelmed by desperation to get far away from Mouthful Mansions.

Tucker got down on this belly and leaned over the side. 'Oh mate, we can't get down there; it's like a well. We'd never get up the other side.' He sounded frantic. 'The water looks black – I can't tell how deep it is and it stinks. Even if we had a rope…we've got no chance.'

The smell of the water was disgusting. It rose up

171

from the bottom of the moat like something had died. It was so wide, too wide to get across.

Tucker sat up and looked back the way they'd come. 'Even if we could chop that down,' he pointed to the nearest tree, 'drag it and throw it over to the other side, I still don't think it would go across the moat.'

'What are we going to do?' Lucas almost screamed at him.

Tucker got up and started pacing up and down the side of the deadly moat. 'I don't know, Larks, I don't know.'

Lucas was half expecting the demons to come charging out of the bushes behind. 'We need to get out of here, they're coming to kill us.'

'I know,' Tucker shouted back. 'You don't have to yell at me, but there's no way we're crossing that moat.'

The boys felt like flies banging against a closed window. They could see their way out to freedom, but no matter how hard they tried they just couldn't make it. Tucker was tapping the bottom of his palm against his forehead as he paced. Lucas looked across to the woods at the other side of the moat again. It wasn't fair. Those villains didn't get to win; they had to find a way to fight back.

'If only we could see…' Lucas started to say, then he punched the air – 'let's climb!'

'Are you mental? We can't be climbing trees, we've got to find a way to get out of here.'

'We need to see,' Lucas said over his shoulder.

He started to climb, not worrying if Tucker was following. Concentrating on getting safely up the tree was calming. He got right up into the top canopy and heard a grunt below; Tucker was right behind him.

There was a good view across the grounds of Mouthful Mansions and no sign of the evil trio.

'Reminds me of that first day', Lucas said, once Tucker was settled, 'when we thought we were the luckiest kids alive.' Keeping Tucker calm would help; if the moat was out then they had to work out another plan. 'The drawbridge is still up,' Lucas added, pointing it out.

They could see the little road snaking away leading to the bigger one. It felt good to watch the toy-like cars trundling along; there was still a world outside all the horror.

'Can't see those demons anywhere.' Tucker was looking all around, but the panic was going from his voice. 'Do you think they've gone back inside?'

Lucas nodded, then thought about it for a bit. 'I bet they never even came outside after us. Leonardo is too fat to run, plus he was hungry, I could tell by the way he was dribbling over that pork.'

'That disgusting pig is always hungry. I didn't think he'd want to eat us though.' Tucker shuddered.

'You do know that I got the mushrooms into the pork, right?'

'What? The Darkest Devils?'

Lucas nodded. 'The question is, will they eat it?'

'Oh, they'll eat it all right. Horrible, greedy... murderers.'

'If they do eat it, then it won't be long before they're asleep.'

'Yeah, that's it! We can creep back in, you can grab the phone from that sleeping fat monster and we'll be home free.'

'Me?' Lucas shuddered, remembering the strength of Leonardo's grip.

'Yes, you. You want to be the hero, don't you, and take the glory? No good if I do all the saving of the world is it?'

'We're in this together, you said it yourself.' Lucas stuck out his hand, unbalancing himself a bit.

'Together,' agreed Tucker, and they shook on it.

Chapter Thirty-One
Darkest Devils

There was no sign of them, or of anything happening. They must have eaten the pork. The boys were in with a chance. It was not light anymore but the real dark hadn't come yet. It felt like they'd been in that tree for ages. They were uncomfortable, thirsty, hungry and beginning to get cold.

'Come on,' Lucas said at last, 'if we're going to do this, let's go.'

It was weird but they didn't feel that scared. It might be because they remembered how the mushrooms had sent them into a deep sleep. Plus, they were finally doing something about trying to escape that didn't mean drowning in a stinking moat.

They climbed down and made their way back, only it was starting to get darker and everything looked and sounded different from before. The trees were thinning out but they were feeling lost.

'Let's climb again.' Tucker found a good tree and from it they could see they were really close to the back of Mouthful Mansions.

'Look!' Tucker was pointing down behind them at a pile of planks leaning up and around the base of a big tree. 'That must be Lady P's hidey. Pathetic.'

Then Lucas spotted Sheba. She was really well camouflaged in a nest of twigs and leaves she had built just a few trees away from them. Lucas tugged at Tucker's sleeve and pointed. The orangutan didn't move.

'She must be sleeping,' whispered Tucker.

Lucas nodded. 'She's so close to Mouthful Mansions. I thought she'd be long gone.'

'Maybe she thinks you're still inside and wants to stay close to you,' said Tucker, 'I know I feel safer there.'

'What in there?' Larks thumbed towards the castle.

'No, you turkey! Next to you; I feel safer next to you.'

'You won't feel safe in a minute.' Lucas said, starting to climb down, but he was smiling. 'Come on.'

Once back at the utility room door the boys pressed their ears against the door. Nothing. They braved it. All the lights were blazing but there was no sound. Lucas could smell the pork so he figured they must've eaten the mushrooms – were they upstairs asleep?

The kitchen was a total mess. There were dirty plates and pans strewn about. Leftover pork was congealing in a frying pan on the hob. There was cutlery and utensils all over the place, even on the floor. It looked like the monsters had eaten then left in a hurry. Every light was blazing. It was bright, but silent. The smell of the pork was strong. Lucas could see Leonardo's enormous plate; the only one of the three that looked like it had been licked clean. They'd eaten the Darkest Devils and were knocked out somewhere.

Cautiously the boys started to tiptoe across the brightly lit studio. Lucas was listening to the blood pulsing in his ears, half-expecting Lady P to come charging in with her gun. He stopped himself from linking his arm up with his friend. Together they tiptoed on towards the double doors. The throne at the head of the banqueting table had someone in it. Feather's coned head was flopped down on top of his gangling arms that sprawled over the table in front of him. A soft whine of breath whistled in and out through his huge beak of a nose. A little wet patch of drool was getting bigger underneath his bony fingers. He was completely gone, but it wasn't Feathers who had the phone. They needed Leonardo and there was no sign of him. They had to keep going.

They crept on, but now that they were back in the house Lucas was properly scared. When they came through the doors they saw Lady P. She was curled up in a tight ball at the bottom of the stairs fast asleep.

Her deerstalker hat was knocked to the side so that it half covered her face. It looked like she must've been on her way to bed but couldn't make it up the stairs. They were made of strong stuff those Darkest Devils. But where was her gun? Was she lying on it? Quietly, the boys went up to her.

'We need the gun,' Lucas mouthed at Tucker.

He nodded and they got close enough to smell her. She smelt stale, a bit like cake you had put in a cupboard and forgotten about. She was even nastier up close and it was scary, like any minute she might jump up and make a grab at them. Tucker bravely knelt down next to her and was checking everywhere around without actually touching her. He nudged her with his knee. Nothing. She was so far gone that even a fog horn wouldn't wake her. Tucker bravely wedged his hands underneath Lady P's body, gave a big shove and rolled her over. She growled like a bear as she turned, then immediately curled up again on her other side. Lucas was impressed by his best friend, but there was no sign of Shaun the shotgun. They had to keep going and risk finding Leonardo without the gun as protection. Tucker got to his feet, and slowly they began to climb the stairs.

'Why everybody sleeping?' boomed a terrifying and familiar voice from the top of the staircase. There, swaying about and waving Shaun in the air above his head was Leonardo De'Largio; the child murderer.

The boys froze. Leonardo lurched dangerously to the side. Lucas willed him to fall down the stairs. The disgusting man looked drunk. He grabbed at the bannister with his free hand and steadied himself. He had a crazed look on his face. His hair was wild, the bright white stripe, usually so neat, ran haphazardly across his head. He shook the gun again and his flabby jowls wobbled.

'What you do?' he demanded.

Lucas thought about the phone in his pocket, begging for it to fall out and tumble down the stairs. They were so close. The other two were fast asleep. Why was he still awake and why did he have the gun? His plate was licked clean; he must've eaten enough to knock out a rhinoceros, yet here he was, still awake.

Part of Lucas raged, angry enough to run up the stairs and cannon ball into the beast's legs. He wanted to knock that evil man down the stairs. He deserved it, but Lucas knew that it would be pointless. It would be like an ant hitting an elephant. He was so enormous, but he looked half gone – if only he would fall.

As if to prove he was still in control, Leonardo took two steps down towards them. Then he brought the gun down onto his shoulder and levelled it to his eye. He looked like a madman.

'Run,' shouted Tucker.

The boys turned, leapt over the curled-up Lady P, just as the first shot rang out, hitting the big oak doors at the front of Mouthful Mansions.

'I kill you,' screamed Leonardo.

Knowing he would, they ran on, past the snoring Feathers. A second shot was fired. Was he coming down the stairs after them? They ran through the

179

messed up kitchen, leaping over scattered cutlery and dropped tea towels.

Leonardo was now shouting in Italian. It sounded brutal. They flew through the door of the utility room and out into the night. As they headed back into the woods another gunshot rang out behind them.

Chapter Thirty-Two

Hiding Out

They ran fast and hard right back into the forest, only now it was dark. Lucas was dazzled by the bright lights of the mansion and couldn't see a thing. He stopped running before he hit a tree and Tucker almost crashed into his back.

'I hate him, I hate all of them,' Lucas spat, glad it was too dark for Tucker to see he was trying hard not to cry. 'Why is he still awake?'

'He's probably too massive for the mushrooms to work properly, but he was pretty out of it.'

'The Darkest Devils were supposed to knock him out. We should have that phone; we should be safe. It was our plan.' Lucas knew he probably sounded like a sulky kid, but he was angry and afraid. Things were looking pretty desperate. It all seemed worse now the daylight had gone.

'We couldn't risk it, not with the gun,' Tucker reasoned. 'He was shooting that thing off all over the place. We were lucky to get out of there alive.'

Tucker got close and even put a hand on Lucas's shoulder.

'Where's Christo gone? Why doesn't he help us? I hate them all and now we're stuck out here in the dark. What's the point of being alive when nobody knows we're here?' Lucas couldn't see a way out. He wanted to feel safe and instead everything was terrifying.

'Come on Larks, this isn't like you. Listen, think about it – we only need to stay alive for tonight.'

'Why just tonight?'

'Don't you remember? Leonardo said the show was going out live for the final week. All those TV vans will arrive in the morning. We just come out of the woods and we'll be saved.'

He'd forgotten all about that. Good old Tucker, what a great mate! That sounded like a much safer plan. Lucas didn't want to go anywhere near Mouthful Mansions ever again. The sight of Leonardo waving that gun around was terrifying. They already knew that the moat was impossible to cross, especially now that it was dark. Much better to sit it out and wait for the TV crew to arrive. Lady P and Feathers were definitely asleep for the night and Leonardo was too drowsy and lazy to come out after them. Who knew where Christo had gone, but it didn't matter; the TV crew would save them. They were far from dead yet.

'We need to make a camp,' Lucas said, instantly brighter. 'Best to be up in a tree, where we can see more. Let's copy Sheba and make a nest.'

'That's more like it!'

Once they were busy, the boys felt less afraid, despite the dark. They weaved smaller branches of the canopy together, then lugged up some sturdy sticks to use as a stronger base between the branches. Finally they camouflaged their nest with leafy twigs, hoping it was well hidden.

They used the torch on Larks's watch when they had to, but were careful in case they were being watched. Tucker found a small pool of water in the mossy roots of their tree, which they sipped at. There was plenty to eat; blackberry bushes, an apple tree and wild sorrel were all growing nearby. The boys gathered what they needed and climbed up into their nest for the night.

The best friends lay on their backs and looked up at the stars. Apart from the light from the moon it was very dark. Now that they were still they could hear all kinds of clicking and rustling, the noises of the wood at night. The trees creaked in the wind and made eerie shapes from their shadows.

'I don't think I'll sleep,' said Larks.

'It might be better if we don't.'

'I feel like I might never sleep again after the things we've seen.' Lucas checked his watch. 'I reckon those vans will be here early, we've only got to stay put for a few hours.'

The boys stopped talking but the growl of Tucker's

stomach kept them company. Lucas looked up at the stars and tried not to listen to all the strange noises below. He thought that maybe Tucker had gone to sleep, so it made him jump when he spoke.

'I keep seeing Miss Downs. You know her face when she peeps round the side of the green chair.'

'Yeah!' Lucas saw it too. 'She looks totally different when you wake her up too early in the morning.'

They chuckled softly.

'Or what about Cook's face when she scrunches it up and calls us, "young horrors" and waves the rolling pin at us,' Lucas said.

Thinking about Brocken House helped to make the dark less scary.

'I wish we had one of Mrs Corneal's big knitted cardigans right now,' said Tucker snuggling down into the nest.

Lucas sniffed a bit to see if he could get Mrs Corneal's smell of lavender but it was just the cold night air that filled his nose.

'I wish Fire Ball was here,' he whispered.

'No', said Tucker, 'what you really wish is that you were there with Flea Bag.'

Lucas snorted a bit and thought about that, then asked, 'Do you think we'll ever get back there, Tucker? Do you think we'll ever get home?'

'I hope so. I thought I never wanted to see that place again and now there's nowhere else I want to be.'

'Me too.'

Eventually the sun began to rise and all the creepy

sights and sounds vanished with the light. Lucas moved to check out the front of Mouthful Mansions. The whole of his body hurt.

'This is what it must be like to be really old,' said Tucker as he uncurled his body. 'I'm dead thirsty.'

Lucas scanned ahead. 'The drawbridge is still up and there's no sign of anybody.'

'Let's go and get a drink,' said Tucker. 'When the vans come, we can run out.'

The boys were so stiff from their night in the nest that climbing down the tree was tricky, but when they got to the bottom the whole wood smelt fresh and alive. Lucas was glad that the water in the mossy pool looked clean in the daylight and drank some. He had just started grazing off the blackberries when Tucker said, 'Shh, listen, that's Lady P.'

Tucker was right. Lady P was still quite far off but there was no mistaking her distant shout. She was awake and she was coming after them.

'I'm out here with Shaun,' she called into the woods. 'You think you can beat me with your silly little mushrooms, but you can't. Vermin must be destroyed and that's what you are.'

'She's the most rubbish hunter ever.' Tucker's voice was quiet.

They crouched low and made their way quickly and quietly back to their tree. Lucas didn't want to go back up, but there didn't seem to be any choice. They climbed to their nest and peeped through the leafy canopy.

'She's there.' Lucas pointed down through the leaves

where he could see her stomping about, flattening the plants in her wake. 'She's going to her hidey,' Lucas whispered. 'She doesn't think we know where it is.'

'Rubbish,' muttered Tucker.

'I know – lucky for us.'

It was a standoff. Lady P was down there and the boys were up in the tree. Nobody moved, not for hours and hours. It was terrifying and exhausting. The boys made desperate checks every few minutes, but the drawbridge stayed up and there was no sign of any TV vans. They eked out the blackberries and apples, but both boys were really thirsty. They had to be silent for hours; the slightest noise could give them away. Lucas swung from feeling totally terrified to wanting to just run at her screaming. It felt as though they would just die up there in that nest; years later someone would find their boy-shaped bones.

Lucas checked his watch for the thousandth time. 'It's nearly six. Something must be wrong,' he whispered.

'Wait. Someone else is coming. It's that chicken freak.'

They heard the call of Feathers across the forest. 'Larissa are you still out here? Where have you been all day? Those boys are fools. Let them rot. Come on in.'

'For goodness sake, Phil!' shouted Lady P stamping out of her hidey, using her gun as a walking stick. 'Don't bellow man, you've blown my cover.'

'Let it go, woman! Leonardo says the boys will just die out here eventually and we can run another competition. We'll get just one child next time. Those two would probably taste rotten anyway, horrible brats.'

Tucker looked at Lucas, his mouth open.

It was unbelievable; they were going to get another kid. Even if they didn't make it those murderers would just keep going with their disgusting plan. They would stop at nothing. Where was the TV crew?

'Alright I'm coming,' Lady P said. 'Is it time then? Have you started the webcams yet?'

'Webcams?' Lucas mouthed at Tucker.

He slapped a palm against his forehead. How could they have been so stupid?

'It's not time just yet,' said Feathers. 'We're almost ready, but come have something to eat first, get yourself tidied up a bit, you've been out here for hours.'

Lady P caught up with Feathers and the boys watched as the two of them walked off together back towards Mouthful Mansions, out of earshot.

'That's why they had cameras in the walls in the studio; they're the webcams,' Lucas said to Tucker.

'That's why the drawbridge is still up,' he agreed, 'and why the TV vans haven't arrived.'

'*Dinners to Die For* is still going out live tonight, but they're using webcams!'

'There'll be no TV crew and it's the last show in the series,' Tucker added.

'We could be stuck out here for the whole winter,' Lucas said. 'Nobody will be back to Mouthful Mansions for another four months.'

Lucas thought about the terror of the day and the cold of the night. The evil monsters were right: Tucker, Sheba and Lucas would die out there for sure.

187

Chapter Thirty-Three

Show Time

How could they survive for four months in the forest? It got so dark and cold, which made everything worse, and the noises were horrible. It had only been a day and a night and already the boys were half-starving and terrified from being hunted all day. What if it snowed? They would never survive. What about Sheba? She wouldn't make it either, but what could they do? If they went back to Mouthful Mansions the monsters would shoot and eat them. Lucas thought about the steep, slippery sides of the moat and its stinking black water. It was an impossible mission to get across it. Tucker was right; they'd die if they tried to cross, because they'd never make it up the steep bank on the other side.

Nobody knew they were trapped in the forest of Mouthful Mansions. Everyone thought they were happy living in Italy. It felt like everything was lost. They were dead if they stayed out in the forest and even more dead if they went back to the castle. Lucas tried not to give up, like he had almost done when the Darkest Devils didn't work on Leonardo. There had to be a way.

'Look,' he said to Tucker, 'the chefs are coming out and Christo is with them too.'

'Leonardo must've talked Christo back round,' said Tucker.

'Whatever he's said to him has worked; looks like they're all mates again. Look, Lady P is even giving Christo her gun.'

'She's pointing out where her hidey is,' said Tucker. 'He's coming this way.'

The three monsters chefs made their way round the corner of the castle whilst Christo began picking his way through the brambles into the forest. Now Lucas was even more confused. The Christo he knew – the one he cooked with, the master baker – would never, he believed, shoot either Sheba or Lucas, and definitely not Tucker; but then there was the other Christo: the bad Christo. He had been with EATS the whole time. For eight years Christo had been killing and cooking endangered animals for those three villains, what was another orangutan to that man? Would he care less about two eleven-year-old boys?

'We can't trust Christo,' Lucas said to Tucker. 'It's

not just his back that's all messed up, those demons have twisted his mind too.'

'Yeah,' agreed Tucker, 'God knows what he's had to do being part of that EATS thing.'

Christo changed direction, heading further into the thick undergrowth, away from the Mansion and the hidey. After watching for a while they lost sight of him.

'Where do you think he's going?' asked Tucker.

Lucas shrugged. 'But…if Christo is out here with the gun,' Lucas said, thinking it through, 'then all three of the murderers are inside without it.'

'Go on,' said Tucker, 'sounds like you've got a plan '

'If we could time it right, then we could run in front of the web cams and…'

'Be on live telly,' finished Tucker, his eyes shining. 'The chefs couldn't touch us! Millions of people sitting in their front rooms would be able to see.'

'You can't hide child murder if it's going out on live TV!'

'Check your watch then, Larks, what time is it?'

Lucas pulled up his sleeve. 'Better check yours too,' he said. 'Let's synchronise.'

'Mine bust ages ago remember?' said Tucker. 'We'll just use yours and stick together.'

'Ok. It's five to six,' Lucas said.

'Right', said Tucker, 'the show goes out at seven thirty, we still have loads of time…hang on…didn't you say it was five to six like, ages ago.'

Lucas checked his watch again, shook his wrist. 'It's stopped! The battery must be dead.' Lucas thought about the times they'd used the torch in the night. Now, when he needed his watch the most, it was broken.

'How are we going to time this without a watch?'

Lucas's heart was thumping in his chest, Tucker was right – without the watch they were in real danger.

'We've got no choice,' Lucas said, 'we have to do this. There's two of us and we're much faster than them, and they've not got the gun any more.'

Tucker looked at his hands, 'I don't know if I can Larks, I mean they want to kill us for real.'

'I know, but we can't stay here. This is our last chance to get out alive.'

Still neither of the boys moved; the thought of having to go back into Mouthful Mansions and face them was truly terrifying.

'If only the vans had come.'

'There's no vans, Tucker. There's only us. We can't wait any longer. We can do this.'

'But I'm scared mate, I'm proper scared.'

'Me too.'

They climbed down the tree as quietly as they could. They'd been watching from above so long that they knew they wouldn't get lost this time, even though things were even more nerve-wracking; more real.

Staying low to the ground, they crept back towards danger. Lucas prayed that Christo could not see them, or wouldn't care if he did, as they made their way out more into the open. The plants were still high, but they were out of the trees now.

The boys found the door into the utility room and

strained to hear what was going on inside. Even though it was pointless, Lucas checked his watch again, which still said just before six. Their timing could be well out, but still they pulled open the door just the tiniest bit. A delicious smell of bread came wafting out, and the boys were so hungry it was enough to entice them inside.

It was brighter in the utility room and they could hear the clink of cutlery on plates and the murmur of voices in the kitchen next door. It was so hard to tell if it was the show or if they were just eating.

Tucker headed straight for the tap and started drinking. Unable to resist the smell of the bread, Lucas opened the cupboard. All the little mounds of dough were rising, but none of it was cooked. Then he spotted a board of cooked rolls and bit into one; instant energy. He watched Tucker. Drinking then seemed more important than anything, it overtook his terror and they swapped places. Once the thirst was gone, Lucas looked around and saw Tucker was bent over into the cleaning cupboard. His best friend emerged with a bottle of toilet cleaner in one hand and furniture polish in the other. The end of a bread roll was sticking out of his mouth.

Armed with cleaning products they bravely neared the kitchen door, listening for a chance to barge in. Then Lucas faintly heard Feathers talking.

'No chicken for our final show, Leonardo?' Can't say that I'm not disappointed.'

He nudged Tucker, 'Now,' he mouthed.

They hurled themselves through the door and ran out into the kitchen.

'We're the winners,' Lucas screamed as loud as he

could. 'We're not in Rome, there is no school, these monsters', he turned to the three chefs who stood huddled round their plates of braised lamb, 'aren't real chefs. They're fakes.'

'Look Larks,' said Tucker, 'some of the cameras are blinking red, the show is on. We're on live telly!'

Lucas saw a red light, it was blinking to the right of the celebrities and there was another one straight ahead. He switched between the two cameras shouting out as loudly as possible. Tucker moved around the room switching on as many other cameras as he could see. Still the chefs did not move.

'These demons tried to eat us,' said Tucker. 'They wanted to cook us up!'

Lucas heard Leonardo laughing but he carried on. 'Don't believe what they say, they're all liars,' he screamed. 'They eat animals for fun and not just any animals, they eat endangered animals.'

'I think that's enough Mr Larks, you said too much, we try to be kind to you, and your friend who cheat to win competition, but you no well, no well in the head and maybe it time to go home,' said Leonardo, and he began waddling towards Lucas.

'They even call themselves EATS,' Lucas shouted ignoring him, not listening to how he was trying to wiggle his way out of it all. 'For the Endangered Animal Tasting Society. They've been doing it for years, eight years.'

'Lucas, the cameras are off,' said Feathers. 'You're talking to yourself.'

Lucas could see all the red lights blinking where

Tucker was turning them on. Feathers was lying – he had to be.

'There are cellars down below me, with a kitchen and cages.' Lucas stamped his foot. 'They put us in one of their cages and they've got a map of all the places where they've eaten endangered animals.'

'And files, Larks,' shouted Tucker waving his toilet cleaner bottle in the air, 'don't forget all the recipes they've used.'

Leonardo snapped his sausage fingers and Feathers got up and walked calmly over to the first camera. Lucas ran after him screaming out, 'We've seen all sorts, whale steaks and mashed monkey, they're monsters. Please come, arrest them, and put them in prison. They're evil.'

Feathers calmly switched off the first camera. Lucas ran towards another one.

'I am Lucas Larks; that's Brian Tucker, we live at Brocken House. We miss it. You have to stop them, they have me and Tucker and they have Sheba, the lost orangutan. They want to eat us all...'

It was the battle of the web cams. Feathers switched them off, Tucker switched them on again whilst the other two watched and Lucas screamed and shouted. Eventually, Lucas was left standing next to Tucker with their sprays in hand as the three monsters started to get nearer. Only one forgotten light kept on blinking.

'You really are pathetically stupid boys,' said Lady P. 'Those cameras were no longer connected; we'd just not turned the dratted things off. The show finished

194

ages ago. Just look at the clock.' Lucas didn't want to look, but had to. A quick glance over his shoulder showed him it was eight fifteen, she was right. Their timing was out; the show had finished at eight. They'd been scoffing rolls when they should've been out there giving their life-saving speech.

'Look at you!' said Feathers. 'Such ridiculous fools. Standing there with a bottle of toilet cleaner and a can of furniture polish. What where you going to do? Clean us to death?'

All three of them burst into laughter, then Lady P came closer. Lucas tried not to panic, but they couldn't run back outside because Christo was out there with the gun. They were cornered. He pretended he had given up, lifting his hands into the air like he had surrendered. Tucker did the same.

'All right,' Lucas said, 'so, we missed our chance. We give up.'

Lady P and Feathers practically ran towards the boys and Lady P reached into her pocket for her bale twine ready to tie them up. The boys let them get close then Lucas pushed down on the nozzle of the polish. Tucker squeezed the toilet cleaner with full force. The toxic chemicals burst out, hitting the two monsters right in their eyes.

They both screamed out in pain. Tucker made for the cameras and started turning them all on again. Leonardo was swaying heavily from side to side. Then Lucas did something he hadn't planned; he called out for Sheba. He screamed out her name loud and clear.

'Sheba, help, we need help,' Lucas screamed over

and over again as loud as he could and all the time Tucker was turning on more cameras. Leonardo lumbered closer, both Feathers and Lady P were screaming and holding their faces and Lucas kept on calling Sheba's name. Lady P wiped the toilet cleaner from her face and came at Lucas like an enraged beast.

'I'll get you, boy!' she was screaming.

Lucas dodged her, still calling out for Sheba. Then they heard her. The orangutan was hammering at the door of the utility room from the outside, but Leonardo was blocking the way. They had to try to move round him to let Sheba in. Lucas remembered his grip; if he got hold of him, he'd be dead. But Lucas was quick, much quicker and smaller than the grotesque Leonardo De'Largio.

'You go,' said Tucker, nodding towards the door.

Lucas got low, ducking and weaving. Lady P made a swipe for him, but Tucker squirted her in the face again. She reeled back, screaming. Lucas got down on all fours and crawled clean through Leonardo's legs. The fat fraud floundered around but he couldn't bend below his waist. His huge hands flapped about but never got close to touching Lucas, who scampered through and opened the door in the utility room to the outside.

In burst Sheba, fierce and triumphant. She hurtled into the kitchen, striking Leonardo down to the floor as if he was nothing more than a skittle. She flew past him and went for Lady P, throwing the disgusting woman against the breakfast bar, knocking her into silence. Next Sheba charged towards Feathers, whooping loudly. The coward was already making for the door running for his life, arms and legs flailing all over the place like a tumble weed. Sheba caught him by the collar and threw him to the floor hard. He knocked his head and was instantly quiet.

The whole place went suddenly silent. Lucas stood in the doorway of the utility room staring at the three evil people sprawled unconscious across the kitchen set. He looked at Tucker, who stood with a bottle of toilet cleaner in his hand staring about him. The little red lights of the cameras blinked on. The huge orangutan suddenly quietened, just like a child after a tantrum. Her breathing slowed and she turned back towards Lucas, becoming smaller and curled inwards once more. She softened quickly from the attacking wild beast, to the animal Lucas had come to know and love when they were locked up together. Boy and ape looked at one another, then she pulled Lucas into her, cuddling and rocking him gently close to her chest. Lucas buried his face in her orange fur.

'Thank you Sheba,' he said, his voice muffled. 'You saved us, you saved our lives.'

Chapter Thirty-Four
Hellos and Goodbyes

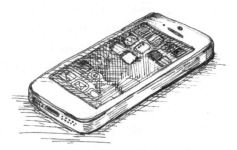

'We need to get his phone,' Tucker said as he stood watching them. 'If the cameras aren't connected then nobody's coming. The evil frauds could wake up and Christo might even come charging back in with the gun.'

Carefully, Lucas prised himself out of Sheba's hug. She kept hold of his arm though. Lucas guessed that she didn't want to be left on her own, so together they made their way over to where Leonardo lay sprawled on his back like a beached whale. They went very slowly. Sheba put her leathery finger on her lips. It was amazing – she was so clever.

Leonardo looked horrible flat out like that, his hair fanned out around him, the white greasy streak curled back and round. Lucas was scared that his little piggy eyes would suddenly open and he would grab his arm and lock on tight, but he had Tucker and Sheba this time, even Leonardo wasn't going to mess with Sheba.

His dinner jacket was undone showing a buttoned-up, straining waistcoat underneath. Lucas flipped his jacket open.

'There's his phone,' Tucker pointed, but he left Lucas to take it out of Leonardo's pocket.

Carefully Larks leaned over the grotesque bulk and eased the phone out. As soon as he had hold of it, the three of them scampered a distance away from the disgusting, unconscious man. He swiped the screen and touched the emergency call button.

A calm woman's voice on the other end asked which service was required.

'Police,' Lucas whispered, then taking in the three unconscious people added, 'and ambulance please, but they'll have to come by helicopter.'

Lucas didn't know whether she'd take him seriously, it all seemed so dramatic, but she was really kind and understanding. She must've heard all sorts of emergencies; perhaps sending out helicopters to stranded kids might've been a normal day's work to her.

'We should tie them up,' Larks suggested and remembered the bale twine that Lady P kept in her pocket.

Together they crept over to where the horrible woman was curled up by the breakfast bar. Lucas had to almost roll her over to get into her pocket but inside was tonnes of the yellow string – and his penknife!

Tucker and Larks quickly bound up all three of the monster chefs' hands and feet.

'Sheba's knocked them out cold,' said Tucker, a touch of awe in his voice.

'I don't care if they're hurt, I just didn't want them getting away,' Lucas said.

Once they were tied up the boys felt a bit safer and so did Sheba because she let go of Lucas's arm. The boys went over to the kitchen and helped themselves to the contents of the fridge. Lucas gave Sheba a huge plastic jug of water that she drank from like a cup. She was awesome.

'We need to get her properly cared for,' said Tucker as he ate.

Lucas nodded. 'We need to get that number from the newspaper. They'll know what to do.'

Tucker went upstairs to get it whilst Lucas tried different codes on Leonardo's phone. He tried all the obvious passcodes: 1234, 4321, 1111, but none of them worked. He stared at the phone, racking his brains. He looked at the numbers and the smaller letters underneath then it came to him: EATS. He typed in the letters for EATS, which were the numbers 3287. He was in!

'Here you go,' said Tucker handing him the newspaper.

Lucas dialled the number printed in the newspaper and put the phone on speaker. Together the boys listened to the ringing on the other end. It was late on a Saturday evening so they didn't expect anyone to answer, but there was a click and then a recorded message started:

Thank you for calling Special Investigations. If you know the extension you require please dial it now. If you would like to report any information in regard to the Importation of Endangered Animals please press 1. If you would like to speak to an operator please hold.

Lucas pressed 1.

A tired-sounding, older woman's voice, with a soft Caribbean accent came on the end of the phone.

'Hello, Special Investigations?'

'Hi,' Larks said. 'Are you the one to speak to about the missing orangutan Sheba?'

'Yes, son, you can speak to me. Do you have any information to help the case?' She sounded doubtful.

'You could say that,' Lucas said and smiled at Sheba. 'I'm looking at her right now.'

There was a pause.

'Hello? Are you still there?' Lucas asked.

'I'm still here, son, and I'm all ears. How about you start by telling me where you both are.'

'We're all at Mouthful Mansions, the home of the celebrity chefs from *Dinners to Die For?* I don't know the address, but it's a massive castle and it's dead famous, I'm sure you'll know how to find us.'

'Is this some kind of joke? Because wasting police time is a serious offence. I can easily trace this call.' She sounded cross and Lucas wondered if she had been given duff information before.

'It's no joke,' said Tucker, 'we're all here. Trace the call, if you like. We're on Leonardo's de'Largio's mobile, but he's out cold on the kitchen floor. Sheba knocked him out. She was brilliant. She saved us.'

'You will look after her won't you? What will you do with her?' Lucas added quickly.

'This is all going a bit fast,' answered the woman, but her voice was softer again. 'I'm going to send out a van from the World Wildlife Fund to collect Sheba. They care about her and want what is best for her, so you don't need to worry. Stay on the phone, won't you? Because, while we wait you can tell me the whole story. How does that sound?'

'It sounds good,' Lucas said. 'Only, just like I told the police and the ambulance people, you'll need to send a helicopter because there's a stinking great moat around the grounds and the drawbridge is up.'

'I'll do that then son; you just hang in there okay? I'm Constance by the way – what's your name?'

'I'm Lucas Larks.'

'And I'm Brian Tucker. We're the boys who won.'

It was all a bit of a whirlwind after that. Constance was great. She stayed on the phone the whole time and listened to everything that had happened. After that first bit when she thought Lucas was winding her up, she believed them. It felt really good to be able to let it all out to someone who listened. Constance was still on the phone when all the people started arriving.

They stayed in the kitchen until they heard the first helicopter. Then they all went over to the windows in the dining room and looked out, even Sheba. The helicopter came swooping over like a huge hover-fly, making the trees sway and the water from the spitting mermaids go all over the place. It landed in the gravelled courtyard and Tucker opened the window to wave at them. More helicopters came and the boys stayed where they were as the rescue teams arrived.

A nice policewoman found them all. She had loads of body armour on and a helmet with a visor as if she was going to calm down crowds at a football match. Lucas let her speak to Constance on the phone and she agreed for him to stay with Sheba. Tucker told her to watch out for any leftover pork because of the Darkest Devils. She smiled and said the forensic team would bag it as evidence.

The people from the World Wildlife Fund were really good. Lucas told them that they didn't need to dart Sheba with that stuff that made her go to sleep because she trusted him. Sheba followed Lucas into her special crate like a little lamb. It was cosy with plenty of room for both of them. Sheba settled down and started eating the pieces of fruit they had left for her. She even passed Lucas a bit of apple to nibble on. They lifted them up together into the helicopter on a big wire because there wasn't enough open space to land all the choppers. Tucker was well jealous because he had to just climb into a helicopter from the ground.

Lucas looked out of the crate, across the courtyard of Mouthful Mansions and saw them lifting up the three evil celebrities laid out on stretchers. They were all still unconscious, police swarming all around them.

They flew Lucas and Sheba back to a wildlife

sanctuary where Constance was waiting. All that time on the phone had made Lucas feel as if he knew her. Constance had an amazing broad smile. The minute she could, Constance took Lucas out of the crate and gave him a really big hug. It felt pretty good.

'You are the bravest kid I've ever known,' she said.

'Hey what about me?'

'And you Tucker, and you mate,' said Constance and hugged him too.

'Get off,' said Tucker.

'He doesn't like hugs,' Lucas said.

'Everyone likes hugs,' said Constance and grinned. 'Now, how about I take you both home?'

They nodded eagerly. Lucas wasn't worried about leaving Sheba. He knew that she was going to be looked after really well, way better than Lucas ever could. And they'd promised that if Larks was given permission that he could visit it her any time at the sanctuary until she was taken back to Sumatra.

'Can we go home in the helicopter?' Tucker asked.

Constance smiled again, 'Is there any other way for Lucas Larks and Brian Tucker to travel?'

Arriving back at Brocken House by helicopter was the best. Way more amazing than when they left by limousine. Even though it was quite late at night, everyone was either outside or gawping from the windows of the old house. The news of what had happened had spread like mad. The helicopter landed in the grounds at the back, flattening all the grass into crazy swirls.

'Watch out for the veggie patch,' Lucas said, but it was too noisy for anyone to hear.

Once landed, Constance helped the boys down. The first person Lucas saw, with her hair all whipped up around her by the helicopter wind was Miss Downs. She hugged Lucas tight and kissed the top of his head. Larks hugged her back, but he wasn't going to kiss her, especially not with Flymo and all the other kids hanging out of the windows watching. She was saying something but the helicopter was too noisy to hear.

Mrs Corneal was there smiling and gesturing for everyone to go inside the house, but on the way Miss Downs grabbed Tucker and pulled him into a tight hug too. Tucker stood there with his arms straight by his sides, but Lucas could see he was grinning.

Chapter Thirty-Five
The Final Show

'Budge up, fatty,' said Tucker launching himself onto the sofa.

'Hey, you're the fat one,' Lucas said, shifting up a bit for him.

'Come on you two', said Miss Downs, 'you know we don't use the word fat at Brocken House. Besides, I can see from here that you're both perfectly proportioned. Now sit down and listen, this is your big moment.'

Lucas smiled at her and watched as the credits came up and the music of *Dinners to Die For* started. *Da, de dah, dah de de dah dah.* A tiny little figure in a combat outfit, instead of Leonardo's disgusting face, appeared on the TV screen:

'Hello, fellow chefs! My name is Lucas Larks, which I used to think was a rubbish name, but now I think it's a good name for a celebrity chef...'

And so it went on, their winning competition entry aired on national television for everyone to see. After the video that Tucker and Larks had made, it was a documentary of the whole horrible story of EATS. It showed everything; Leonardo announcing the competition; the letter of congratulations; an interview with the hired limo driver; their bedrooms at Mouthful Mansions; behind the scenes of the kitchen, the cellars and secret kitchen with all the horrible ingredients; the leg chain they used; the cages and all the folders of recipes.

The documentary showed some of the footage the web cams had recorded; Lucas shouting about what had happened; Tucker running about turning all the cameras on; the chefs being sprayed in their eyes; Larks ducking under Leonardo's tree-trunk legs and Sheba roaring in and knocking them all unconscious.

It followed with news reports of when all three of the monster chefs were arrested, all the secret underground operation of EATS and how they imported all the animals.

The last part was the saddest and the happiest because it was all about Sheba's recovery to get her ready to be released back into the wild.

At the end of the programme they flashed up a telephone number for people to call if they wanted to make a donation to a charity to help save endangered animals and another one for children in care – kids just like Larks and Tucker. It was a brilliant documentary – they didn't leave anything out.

'Wow,' said Miss Downs, switching off the telly and turning to the friends. Lucas could feel himself blushing as she stared at him, smiling. 'What can I say except, wow? You two are the bravest eleven, sorry twelve-year-olds, that I have ever known and I've known one or two.'

'Yeah, well,' said Tucker, 'I liked it when they showed our nest and compared it to Sheba's.'

'Do you remember the cold? It was a really long night.'

'I bet it was, you poor things,' sympathised Miss Downs, 'and here we were, all thinking you were in Rome cooking your little hearts out.'

Tucker and Larks shared a look; so relieved it was all over. It was only a few months ago and yet it felt like a different lifetime.

'I'm so glad that you'd got those cameras back on, Brian,' she said. 'Even though they weren't broadcasting any more we still got all that evidence.'

'Good effort, *Brian*,' Larks said and Tucker punched him on the arm.

'They can use all that in the courts can't they Miss Downs?' Lucas asked.

'Yes, they can,' she said.

Larks was relieved. Those evil criminals had to go to prison and stay there. Forever.

'Funny about Christo though isn't it? That they never found him, even after they found the gun,' Lucas said. 'I mean, there was no way he could get across that moat, so I don't know how he got away. Nobody ever saw him and he never had any documents. I don't think anyone believes that he was real, but yet we saw him every day, didn't we Tucker?'

'Christo…? Hmmm…?' Tucker was shaking his head and looking at the floor, 'Nope, I got nothing.'

It was Lucas's turn to punch Tucker on the arm for that one, but Tucker punched Lucas right back without even blinking.

'You two are impossible,' said Miss Downs but she was laughing. 'This might sound unprofessional of me, but in a funny way I'm glad that it didn't work out because now you're back home with us at Brocken House.'

'Oh, it will take more than a bunch of child murderers to scare us away, Miss Downs,' said Tucker. Just at that exact moment Tucker shot up out of his place on the sofa like he'd been electrocuted.

'Flea Bag,' he whined to the cat that had jumped onto the arm beside him. FB ignored Tucker and happily padded his way over to Lucas for a fuss. 'You scared me half to death.'

They laughed then, proper belly laughs, and it felt good to be home.

Author Warning

Luckily there's no such thing as Darkest Devils, but wild mushrooms can be extremely dangerous, please DON'T pick them.

Hip Hip Hoorays

Leonardo De'Largio and the idea for the book first came to me in 2002 when I was living in Sheffield and part of a 'writing for children group' led by the marvellous, Leah Fleetwood. I also shared my early writing with a class at Nethergreen Junior School through a Y6 teacher friend, Trevor Thornton.

Life got in the way and I didn't come back to the story for many years. When I did pick it up again I received further help from KC Critterati, SCBWI & VW members, and my fabulous daughters Fay and Sasha.

Throughout the many drafts I have always listened to, and acted on, the thoughts and opinions of kids.

Thanks to everyone who has helped create EATS and a special thank you goes out to the talented Annie Harris, for her wonderful illustrations and never-ending support.

About The Author:
Camilla Chester

You want to know about me? How many of you went straight to this page? If you don't like the sound of me, there's no chance you're buying or reading the book – is that right?

Pressure!

I write books for kids because my own love of reading started when I was young and I want to try and give that feeling to others. I also think animals are amazing. How's that?

Oh, and after reading the book you might want to know that no, I'm not strictly a vegetarian, although I do believe we need to think about what we eat because it really does affect our wonderful planet Earth.

EATS is my second book. My first, *Jarred Dreams*, was published in 2016 and my third book, *Thirteenth Wish* will be out soon.

If you'd like to know more about me and my books please take a look at my website: www.camillachester.com

Did you enjoy this book?

Reviews are like tips for authors. Please leave a tip for
Camilla Chester by rating and/or reviewing *EATS* at
Amazon.co.uk.
Thank you!